THE AMBUSHERS

Hanson levered the rifle. "I'm going to give them a little taste of their own medicine!" He put the barrel through the window and let go until the weapon was empty.

"You're wastin' bullets!" Slocum cried.

Hanson started to say something, but he never got the chance. Several slugs ripped through the windows, tearing into his body. Blood began to pour from his chest and stomach.

The woman fell across the seat, grabbing at Slocum's legs. "Do something! Don't let him die."

Slocum pushed her back. "That's outta my hands . . ."

JAKE LOGAN

SLOCUM AND THE
TIN STAR SWINDLE

BERKLEY BOOKS, NEW YORK

SLOCUM AND THE TIN STAR SWINDLE

A Berkley Book / published by arrangement with
the author

PRINTING HISTORY
Berkley edition / July 1993

All rights reserved.
Copyright © 1993 by The Berkley Publishing Group.
This book may not be reproduced in whole or in part,
by mimeograph or any other means, without permission.
For information address: The Berkley Publishing Group,
200 Madison Avenue, New York, New York 10016.

ISBN: 0-425-13811-9

A BERKLEY BOOK ® TM 757,375
Berkley Books are published by The Berkley Publishing Group,
200 Madison Avenue, New York, New York 10016.
The name "BERKLEY" and the "B" logo
are trademarks belonging to Berkley Publishing Corporation

PRINTED IN THE UNITED STATES OF AMERICA

10 9 8 7 6 5 4 3 2 1

Dedicated to R. L. Barfield

1

John Slocum was tired as hell of Cheyenne in springtime. The lanky rebel from Georgia had only been around the town for three days, but he was almost ready to leave the muddy streets and the hateful wind that swept through the cracks in the stable where he had been sleeping. Rain had dripped on him for the better part of two nights, leaving him sore and short-tempered. Slocum would have been on a trail out of Wyoming if not for a certain woman who had not yet appeared for the evening. Slocum kept his green eyes darting back and forth, awaiting the shifting curves under the red dance-hall dress.

"You want another one, cowboy?"

Slocum glanced up to see a sad-faced girl with dirty blond hair. She knew what he was waiting for. There were a half dozen men, cowboys, and soldiers waiting for the same thing. Slocum probably didn't have a chance, but something was making him stay and try.

"I mean, this is a saloon, cowboy," the girl said. "Not much a' one, I know, but we got to hide way out here on the prairie because of the army. Them generals get righteous, even though most of 'em been here to try Ladybell."

Slocum didn't want her to talk anymore. He nodded at the shot glass in front of him. She filled it, Slocum hit it, she filled it again, and he paid her, leaving the full shot in front of him. When the girl left, Slocum leaned back, watching the stairs for Ladybell's entrance.

Slouching in the chair, John Slocum looked like any other trail rider. From the crest of his wide-brimmed hat to the thin soles of his boots, he resembled a spook that had swirled out of a prairie dust cloud. The color of his shirt had faded long ago and his denim trousers could stand alone if propped against a tree. She would probably complain that he hadn't bathed for a while, but he still had to give it a run.

Slocum shifted in the chair, touching the butt of the weapon that hung on his side. He was carrying an old Navy Colt that he had bought the day before, trading a Peacemaker for the .36 caliber pistol that had been converted to cartridge. The gunsmith had also given him some money in the trade, leaving Slocum flush for the moment.

The Peacemaker had been a fine weapon, but when Slocum saw the woman in the red dress, he had to find money somehow. She was a whore, true, but there was a time when a man had to waste everything just for that one little pleasure to be remembered—until the next chippy.

He sipped half the whiskey, thinking that it would be easy to leave. His horse, a strong pinto, was tied out in back of the saloon. He could just climb in the saddle and ride away without looking back. Hell, the sheriff had been eyeing Slocum, probably trying to match the description with a wanted poster. Slocum couldn't remember if he had any paper on him in Wyoming.

But he couldn't just ride off without trying. The woman was in his head, crawling around like a crawdaddy under a rock, driving him *loco*. He saw her face when he fell back on the damp hay, remembered her first thing in the morning after his eyes opened. She was a whore, she could be bought. But did he have enough?

Slocum reached into the pocket of his dusty leather vest. He took out five double eagles: his life savings, thanks to the gun money. One hundred dollars. Something inside told him that he would have to spend it all. Women like Ladybell took everything they could and then some.

"Here, cowboy."

The girl was there again, filling his glass to the rim. Slocum frowned at her. He didn't like being hustled for liquor.

She seemed to read his thoughts. "On the house."

His face slacked into a suspicious expression. "What for?"

"On account of you bein' here the past two nights, gawkin' at Ladybell like the rest of these prickly cowpokes. You bought your share and didn't try to chisel me for free ones."

"I ain't much on charity," Slocum said. "Givin' or receivin'."

The dirty blonde smirked at him. "You're a real riled-up Reb. I bet your name is Johnny. Johnny Reb."

"I don't want no free whiskey." He pushed the shot away. "Take it."

"It's from Ladybell," the girl replied with a grin. "You still want me to take it away?"

Slocum's chest had tightened suddenly. Ladybell? Why would she want to buy him a drink? The girl was pulling his leg.

"Suit yourself," she told him. "I'll take it if you—"

Slocum pushed her hand away as she reached for the shot glass. He picked it up and knocked back the burning pop skull. He was sick of Wyoming. It was time to cut his losses and ride the hell out of Cheyenne, get south to some warmer place, to a few dry spots. He stood up, stretching his lanky frame until his head almost scraped the rafters of the cheap saloon-whorehouse.

"Sure you don't want to wait?" the girl asked him.

Slocum shook his head. He had fretted enough over the whore. It was time to get moving before he landed himself a night in jail for some petty grievance wherein a local lawman refused to have a sense of humor.

"No tip?" the girl said with a hostile tone.

"Don't never stand directly in back of a mean horse," Slocum replied.

He started to move past her, but he never took a full step. His green eyes caught a glimpse of red in the shadows of the staircase. Ladybell took the last step down with the slightest jiggle. Slocum was frozen, stunned by her garish siren's entrance.

Slocum eased back into his chair, keeping his gaze on the brunette in the red taffeta dress. "Bring me 'nother whiskey."

The waitress girl sighed. "They all come for Ladybell. A homely girl ain't got a chance 'round here."

"Just bring me the whiskey," he said blankly.

Ladybell naturally stopped at the bottom of the staircase, posing for all eyes to see. Every head in the place turned toward her. Slocum wasn't the only one who wanted her.

There'd be a line outside her room tonight, if she took them on. Rumor had it that Ladybell chose her own, charged big money, and then told the rest to go yank it in a croaker sack or call on one of the lesser girls in the brothel.

For a moment, her dark eyes fell on Slocum. Her pouty lips parted and turned upward with the vaguest smile. She began to move forward, her full figure gliding between the tables. She wasn't the youngest filly in the barn, but she had held up well. Well enough to make Slocum hang around for his long-shot chance.

He threw back the whiskey and started to finger the gold coins in his right hand. "Damn her. She could get it all if she'd choose me."

Didn't they always get it all?

He focused on the vermillion vision. Ladybell had alit at a table where they were dealing faro. Slocum fought the urge to go sit in on the game. He reached into his pocket for his tobacco pouch and spun a wet handroll. The girl brought him a match and another shot of hooch.

Ladybell even looked pretty through the cloud of smoke. A hundred dollars. Was she worth it? Would she even take the money? She might not want to bed down with a stinking trail bum for any amount of gold.

She rose again. Slocum squinted through the smoke. She sashayed between more tables, heading for the rough counter that served as a bar. There was a soldier standing there, an older gentleman. Definitely an officer, Slocum thought. Ladybell began to laugh at him, keeping her face turned away from the lanky rebel.

How could she have ended up here? Slocum wondered. Maybe she had suffered some bad luck along the way. A few setbacks could change things in a hurry. Setbacks like hanging around a two-bit army town, waiting to waste everything on an aging chippy who just happened to look damn fine in red.

"More whiskey, cowboy. On Ladybell."

The dirty blond woman poured him a full shot glass. When he downed it, she gave him another. Slocum was starting to feel the liquor. His head didn't seem to be balanced on his neck.

"Ladybell's private stock," the girl went on. "It don't burn like that Colorado rotgut. Here, take it."

"Might as well," Slocum replied. "Fill it. I ain't gonna see no action tonight."

"Don't be so sure of that, sir!"

The voice did not belong to the girl. Slocum glanced up to see that Ladybell was standing behind the waitress. Her perfume filled the air around Slocum, like fresh Georgia honeysuckle.

Slocum immediately took off his hat and put it on the table. He looked back at Ladybell with no expression on his countenance. He knew he had to wait her out. Women could be like wild horses, show no fear, keep a steady hand, and you might get to ride them one day.

"Leave us alone, Dottie," Ladybell said in her husky tone. "And leave the bottle."

The girl poured Slocum another blast and rested the bottle in front of him. Ladybell eased into a chair across the table, posing like a fancy woman from Denver or San Francisco. Her smile could have melted an ice-capped peak.

"Might I inquire as to your name, sir?" she asked.

Slocum shifted nervously in his seat. "John."

"John. Yes."

The cowboy's gut was churning, his legs were weak. He hadn't expected her to fall right into his lap. It was killing him. The perfume alone was enough to make a man keel over dead.

Ladybell kept herself in the shadows, trying to hide the lines and wrinkles. "You aren't comfortable with talking, are you John?"

"No, ma'am."

"And you're wondering why I came over to your table, aren't you? Why I broke out my private stock of whiskey?"

"Yes'm."

"A Southern gentleman. I can tell. Did you fight for Dixie?"

Slocum nodded. "I did."

Ladybell laughed. "How noble. I, too, hail from Dixie, a godforsaken Alabama town that I'd just soon forget."

Slocum suddenly found himself leaning toward her. "Did the Yankees ruin your family too?"

She laughed louder. "No, Mr. John. My family was ruined long before the Yankees ever got there."

Slocum couldn't bring himself to laugh at her little joke. In another life, they might have been in different worlds, stuck in that hierarchy of the Old South. But here in Wyoming, in the cathouse, they were simply whore and customer. The war had made it so.

"What part of Dixie you hail from, Cowboy John?"

"Georgia."

"What part of Georgia?"

"Just Georgia."

Ladybell eyed him curiously. "No more talking, huh? What you want to do? Get down to business? Are you like all the rest?"

Slocum sighed. "No'm, I was just wonderin' what I could do to honor a fine daughter of Dixie like yourself."

"Aw, that's sweet. You want to go upstairs?"

Slocum swallowed, trying to clear his dry throat. It had happened so fast. He had dreams like this on the trail. One minute she was nowhere to be seen, the next second she was offering herself to him.

"I ain't sure I've got enough," Slocum said. "You're s'posed to come dear."

Ladybell grinned. "Oh, I do."

"How much?" he asked cautiously.

"Everything you got in your pocket," she replied. "Everything."

"I knew it."

She drew a hand over the bare white skin of her exposed bosom, mocking him with a girlish giggle. "Can you stand it?"

He sighed. "I can stand it. Only—I ain't had a bath in a while."

She touched his forearm, driving him out of his skin. "A bath comes with the bed. And I keep you all night. You got to make me feel good too."

Slocum looked at the five golden coins in his right hand. It was a lot to give up. He could've just gotten on his pinto and headed away from Cheyenne. But he didn't.

"I'm gonna show you a night you're never gonna forget," Ladybell said. "I'll take you up and down the ladder twice. I'll do things you ain't never thought of and you'll do the same to me."

Slocum could feel his rigid member growing inside his dusty jeans. He had no memory of ever wanting a woman the way he wanted this one. And she was talking dirty, abandoning the fancy-woman talk for the backwoods twang of an Alabama farm girl who had not been so lucky along the trail.

"You still ain't told me one thing," Slocum said.

"What?"

He shrugged. "I'm the dirtiest rider in here. I thought you'd go with that army officer. Why'd you go for me?"

"Cause I can see how hungry you are, cowboy. And you're tall, you got big feet. I'm bettin' that you got a Johnson the size of a pregnant rattlesnake. Are you ready to strike?"

Where the hell had she learned to talk like that? She was beautiful in the dim light. Curly brown hair, soft white skin, the red dress, a mouth that spoke the language a desperate man wanted to hear. Slocum hadn't purchased many high-falutin whores in his time, but Ladybell had to be at the top of the list.

"Give me a minute to freshen up," she said in a hoarse whisper. "Then you come on. Third door on your left."

"I can find it."

He would just follow the trail of her perfume.

Ladybell got up and sashayed slowly toward the stairs. She lingered a moment by each table, flirting in a way that made Slocum deathly jealous. Men killed each other over lesser women. A whore like Ladybell could leave a lot of corpses in the halls of the cathouse.

She began to ascend the stairs, stopping to look back at Slocum. The other hopeful whoremongers saw that she was gazing at the tall, dirty, green-eyed drifter. He wondered if he would have to fight any of them.

"You want another drink?" asked the blond girl named Dottie.

Slocum nodded. "As long as it's on the house."

"Ladybell'll clean you dry," the girl warned.

"I don't care."

Dottie sat down in the same chair that had been occupied by the brunette madam. "I'll take you on for three dollars."

Slocum gazed into her desperate eyes. "What?"

"Three dollars. Here, look."

She stood, lifting the hem of her stained, flour sack dress. "You want to touch it?"

Slocum waved her off. "Get gone."

Dottie sat down, lowering her dress. "Ladybell has a boy-friend. His name is Johnny Pike. He's playin' cards tonight back in town. If he finds out you been with Ladybell, he'll want to fight you."

Slocum grimaced. "You're makin' it up."

"I ain't lyin'. Johnny is the jealous kind. He's killed more'n one man over Ladybell."

Slocum didn't want to hear it. He was going to pay, plain and simple. Whores didn't have boyfriends, or if they did, the friend had to be really understanding. A working woman could make a man think she belonged to him, but when it came to the next customer, she was right there with her hand out.

"Three dollars!" Dottie urged.

Slocum stood up. "I got company to keep."

He moved past her, heading for the stairs. The perfume hung like fog in the air. The other patrons of the saloon-cathouse glared enviously as the tall man passed them. Why had he been the lucky one?

Slocum kept his eyes darting back and forth to make sure no one wanted to try his gun hand. He reached the stairs without a challenge. Third door, he said to himself. She was going to be ready for him.

As he started to climb, the voices rose in the shadows.

"Lucky bastard!"

"Why'd she give it to him?"

"I brought my money tonight."

"Ladybell's funny, she don't always choose the one you might think."

"Lucky bastard!"

"Maybe we'll get another shot tonight."

"No, when Ladybell chooses, that's it."

Dottie listened to them, watching as Slocum disappeared upstairs. "That damned bastard. I'm good enough for him. If Johnny Pike hears about this—"

Dottie's dull eyes brightened a little. She reached for the strings of her ratty apron. Johnny Pike was going to hear about Slocum. Dottie decided to go into Cheyenne to tell him!

2

Slocum eased himself down into the steaming water of Ladybell's private tub. She poured a bucket of cooler liquid over his head. The splash was scented like lilacs. Ladybell put her hands on Slocum's hair and started to work up a rich white lather.

"You don't have any lice," she said. "That's good for a change."

Her hands worked his upper half, sliding along his neck to his shoulders and then his chest. She had skill in her fingers. She hadn't even touched his pecker yet and he was as primed as a cap and ball pistol.

Her voice dropped to a timid whisper. "You must ride a lot. I like a man lean. Clean and lean. You got that money?"

Slocum pointed to his denim pants. "Right pocket."

Ladybell snapped her fingers. A shadow appeared in the doorway. Slocum tensed. Was it a trap? He had been so ready for the other thing. . . .

She put her hand on his shoulder. "It's only Lin Ching. He works for me. Don't worry, we're okay."

A small Chinese man ambled into the room, picking up Slocum's dirty clothes. "I get clean, Miss Ladybell. You have tomorrow."

"Thanks, Lin Ching. Tell Dottie to give you some brandy."

"I get clean."

Slocum eyed the Chinaman until he was out of the room. "I want my duds back. I ain't leavin' without 'em."

She dipped her hands into the tub and massaged his soapy shoulders again. "I'd trust Lin Ching before I'd trust myself. Besides, it's all part of the service. A queen needs a king. I'm treating you like a king tonight, John. And you'll treat me like a queen."

"If you say so."

Her hands left him for a moment. Slocum heard the rustle of falling taffeta. When she knelt down again, he felt her soft breasts brushing against his back. Her nipples hardened at the touch. Slocum started to reach back for a good feel.

Ladybell stopped him. "No, not yet. Let's take it slow. I need a little more time to get going."

Slocum nodded, lying back in the tub. He was trying to stay calm, but it was hard now that she was naked. Her hands returned, exploring his chest and stomach. He thought he was going to explode when she stroked his thighs. She touched everything but his Johnson.

"How long do I got to wait?" he asked.

After all, he was paying good money! He deserved to get what he wanted. She was trying to make him surrender completely.

"Patience is a virtue," Ladybell replied, "Even though neither one of us has any real virtue at all."

She drew back her hands and told Slocum to get out of the tub. He obeyed her. As soon as he was out she climbed in, reaching for another handful of fancy powdered soap.

"Now you're going to wash me," she said. "Go ahead. You can touch me now. Touch anything you want."

He knelt beside her, dipping his hands in the water. She guided him toward her breasts.

"Yes," Ladybell moaned. "Touch me there."

Next, his fingers probed the thick lips of her femininity. Ladybell guided him again. She put his index finger on the spot that felt good. Slocum worked his fingertip back and forth, causing her to splash in the tub.

"Oh, you do know how to make a girl feel good," she said, smiling up at him. "Now, let me make you feel good. Back in the tub, John Cowboy."

Slocum trembled as he climbed back into the hot water. She was driving him *loco*. Was he ever going to get it?

"Now, let's see what you've got down there," Ladybell cooed. "We've got to make sure you're clean all over."

"You're takin' your good time, woman!" Slocum blurted out.

She faked a beautiful pout. "I thought y'all was a Southern gentleman, Mr. John Cowboy. A true son of the Confederacy."

"I am," Slocum replied. "And we'll do it for Dixie if you want. But let's just by God do it!"

Her hands dived beneath the water. Slocum felt her grip his erect member. She jerked him up and down for a moment.

"Umm," Ladybell said. "I can see I made the right choice. You're hung like a Fort Laramie mule."

Slocum felt the sap rising. "Doggone it, Miss Ladybell, I don't think I can wait another second."

"You know something? Neither can I."

She came over the side of the tub, straddling his body. Her hand reached again for his member. In a smooth motion, she sat down, taking him inside her. Her thick body began to splash up and down.

Slocum cupped her breasts, releasing inside her as soon as he held the soft mounds of flesh. His whole body and spirit seemed to flow into her. Ladybell laughed and leaned over to kiss him.

The woman sat up, rocking on him even as he went limp. "Oh, we're not done, not by a tinker's mile."

He wondered what else she was in the mood for.

"Let's dry off and get into bed," Ladybell said.

When they were out of the tub, Slocum grabbed her, pulling her into his body, and loving the way she felt against his skin. They kissed for a long time, until she broke away and lay back on the bed, spreading her thick thighs. The dark patch between her legs was inviting him again.

Slocum was ready too.

"You got hard again in a hurry," Ladybell mocked. "That thing is swellin' like a rattler bite."

Slocum fell on top of her, prodding madly. She accepted him, wrapping her legs around his waist. Slocum held on for his life as she began to shake. He thought the bed was going to crash through the floor to the saloon below.

Ladybell shivered and then grabbed his shoulders. "Don't shoot," she gasped. "Not yet."

She rolled him off her. Slocum lay back, watching her. He couldn't imagine what she must have in mind. Then he heard the other woman moving in the shadows of the bedroom.

"Carlita," Ladybell called.

"Si, *señora*."

She grinned at Slocum. "Mind if she joins us?"

Slocum shook his head. The Mexican girl climbed into bed with them. She was petite, small-breasted, and smelled slightly of peppers. Ladybell began to kiss the Mexican girl on the mouth.

"Damn," Slocum said.

Ladybell glanced up at him. "What?"

"I was just thinkin'," he replied slowly, "that this sure as hell is worth a hundred dollars."

Ladybell laughed. "You'll never miss the money, cowboy. Now, what say we kiss this sweet thing."

Dottie, the dirty blond girl from Ladybell's place, reined up a stubborn mule behind a dark building on the north side of Cheyenne. Everybody knew about the poker game going on in the old shack. Even some of the bigwigs from the army post played there. Nobody seemed to mind gambling in town, it was just whoring that had become less tolerable to the citizens. Ladybell had to keep her house a good distance away so nobody would holler.

Dottie tiptoed toward the doorway hoping that Johnny Pike's men would be waiting outside. But they weren't there. And Dottie did not know the man who was standing guard. She would just have to take her chances. She came out of the shadows and strode bravely toward the sentry.

"Just hold it right there," the man said.

Dottie stopped and put her hands on her hips. She heard the faint clicking of a pistol cylinder. The sentry had actually drawn on her.

"I got to see Johnny Pike," Dottie said.

The man dropped his gun into its holster and shook his head. "Nobody's goin' in there."

"I got to see him," Dottie whined. "I'll do it with you."

He rubbed his chin, looking her over. "Nope, I'm savin' my geetus for Miss Ladybell."

"That's who this is about," Dottie replied. "I got news for Johnny about Ladybell. You got to let me in."

The man's face suddenly turned white, as if he were afraid. "Listen, don't you tell Johnny I been savin' up for a roll with Ladybell."

Dottie smiled wickedly. "So, you're afraid of Johnny."

"I ain't no such—"

"I'm gonna tell him, unless you let me in," she kept on. "I mean, do you really want to be the one that held back news of Ladybell? Johnny won't like that one bit."

He thought it over. "Okay, go in. But you better not tell him I said what I said about Ladybell."

"I won't."

Dottie pushed through the tattered cloth curtain that covered the doorway. Six men were hunched around a table with cards in their hands. A dim lantern was the only light over the gamblers. Dottie squinted, searching for Johnny's face. He was a good-looking kid who always wore a black leather hat. She found him sitting behind a jackpot full of winnings.

"Johnny!"

He looked up quick, as did the others.

"Johnny, it's me, Dottie, from Ladybell's place."

"Get her the hell out of here," said one of the players.

Johnny gazed worriedly at the girl. "What's wrong?"

Dottie decided to lie it up big. "It's Ladybell," she said. "One of her old beaus showed up from Alabama. They're together now at the saloon, upstairs. He claims he's going to marry her and said he'd kill anyone who tries to stop him."

Johnny's face turned bright red. "That son of a—"

He started to bolt up from the table.

"Hey, you ain't goin' nowhere, Pike," said an irate gambler.

"Yeah, you're ahead, Johnny," moaned another. "You got to give us a chance to get some of it back."

Johnny glanced around the table. They were all glaring at him. A couple of them had their hands on their gun butts. If he decided to leave with his winnings, he might have to kill a couple of them.

"Damn it!" He grunted like a bear. "I won't be gone long, boys."

"Sit down, Pike."

"Yeah, don't chisel us."

"We got a right!"

Johnny was aware of the code. They had agreed to play all night and it wouldn't be right if he left early. He had to give them a break before he went and killed the man who was in bed with Ladybell.

"All right," Pike muttered. "I'll stay."

Dottie smirked as he sat back down. "Don't worry, Johnny, she's going to keep him up there all night."

Johnny wanted to leave again, but the others wouldn't let him. He had to stay and roll the cards. Then he planned to head out to the cathouse to roll Ladybell and her soon-to-be-dead lover.

Slocum awoke with a start, sitting up in bed next to the woman. Ladybell was on her stomach, spread out on the feather mattress. The Mexican girl was gone now. It all seemed like a waking dream to the pie-eyed drifter.

He reached out to touch the curve of her exposed hip. His finger played along the ridge of her buttocks. She was a woman with appetites beyond his own. But she hadn't worn him out completely.

Ladybell began to squirm under his hand. She rolled over and spread her legs. Slocum climbed between her thighs, riding slow at first and then hastening toward the climax. Ladybell was exhausted before he rolled off her nearly an hour later.

Slocum sat on the edge of the bed, listening to the quiet darkness. The house was quiet. Ladybell supposedly had three other girls who took care of the losers in the nightly contest for the madam's favors.

Somewhere in the house, a clock struck five times. Slocum could see the first hints of dawn on the windowpane. It wouldn't be light for a while, but the day was ready to begin.

Stepping to the window, he looked down at his mount which was still tied behind the house. He could go any time. He had been with the woman and she had been worth it. Now he had to get the hell out of Wyoming.

Slocum's head jerked away from the window. He heard something in the other room where the bathtub sat. Someone was moving around. Slocum groped at the headboard of the bed until he found his .36 Navy Colt. He thumbed back the hammer and started for the bathroom.

There wasn't enough light to actually see the intruder, but Slocum knew he was getting closer. Shuffling feet moved across the dusty floor, scraping loud enough for the lanky rebel to pinpoint the bushwhacker. Slocum jumped out of the shadows and stuck the .36 barrel on the back of the intruder's neck.

"Move slow or they'll be sweepin' up your head."

Immediately, the man began to chatter in Chinese, awakening Ladybell. She called to Lin Ching. Slocum let go of the Chinaman.

"Caught him sneakin' up on me," he said.

"I just bring clothes!" the Chinaman insisted.

"It's all right, Lin Ching," Ladybell said. "Just hang them over there."

Slocum kept the gun in hand until the grousing Chinaman had gone. As he slipped it back into the holster, he felt Ladybell's fingers on his member. She started to tug at him.

"You got another one in you?" she asked.

Slocum lay down next to her. "I ain't sure."

Ladybell's head dipped toward his groin. "Let me see what I can do. Maybe I can suck it back to life."

Slocum knew he never should have doubted her. It was one of the few times he had ever gotten his money's worth. She knew how to please a man.

"Do it again."

He gave it another try, entering her. But he could not climax again. She had drained most of his sap. Ladybell used him to do a lot of other things that they had not done before.

"I hope we meet again in heaven," Slocum muttered when they stopped.

Ladybell laughed. "Heaven? What makes you think I'm gonna be up there with old St. Peter?"

"You showed me a little heaven tonight," the rebel replied. "Besides, St. Peter's a man. He'll want to know you. Take my word for it."

Ladybell stretched catlike in the bed, sighing blissfully. "Been a while since I've had it like that. Most of these boys are on and off. They can't keep up with me."

I ain't sure I can! Slocum thought to himself.

She gazed at the glow on the window. "Look, it's gettin' light. Listen!"

The clock was striking six in the hollows of the cathouse.

Slocum wanted to rest a while longer, to sleep off some of the liquor and the poking. He hadn't seen a feather mattress in a damned long time. It was almost too soft, like a cloud in the blue sky.

"Mind if I get some shut-eye?" he asked.

Ladybell giggled. "Sleep all you like. I'm going to keep you around for a while. We can play. Would you like that?"

"I gotta sleep on it," Slocum replied.

His face went into the plush pillow. He drew up the comforter to warm his naked body. He was almost asleep when a loud ruckus arose in the house. He sat up to hear a man screaming at the top of his lungs.

"Oh no," Ladybell said. "Johnny Pike. Damn him! He doesn't own me!"

Slocum shook his head. The girl had not been lying. Ladybell did have a jealous beau. And Slocum could hear him clomping up the stairs.

"I think you'd better go," Ladybell whispered.

Slocum figured she was right.

3

Slocum tried to move quickly in the dark, gathering his possessions for a window exit. He couldn't see and Ladybell kept getting in his way. He ripped his clothes from the wall where the Chinaman had hung them to dry. Grabbing his boots with his left hand, he used his right to carry the Colt where it could be drawn in a hurry.

Ladybell put his hat on top of his head. "Take care of yourself, John Cowboy. Make sure you come back to see me."

"Write it in the Good Book," Slocum replied.

He started for the window.

Johnny Pike's fists began to punish the doorway. "Bell, you *loco* woman, open this door! Who you got in there?"

Ladybell opened the window for Slocum. "Nobody, honey. Just a minute. I'll let you in after I put my face on." To Slocum she whispered, "Hurry!"

Johnny's shoulder tried the door. The door buckled but it didn't give. Slocum stuck one leg out the window, feeling for the roof of the back porch.

"Bell, I know you got your beau from Alabama in there!" Johnny cried.

"No, honey—wait a minute? Alabama!"

Slocum's bundle of clothing caught a loose splinter that caused him to hesitate half in and half out of the casement. "Ladybell, get me loose!"

She reached for the splinter. "Hold on, Johnny! I'll be right there."

The shoulder battered the door again. It held once more but then broke open on the next shove. Johnny Pike cried out like a Shoshone warrior when he saw Slocum stuck in the opening.

"Shit!" Slocum grunted.

Johnny went for his sidearm. Slocum tried to get the Navy in hand but the angle was wrong. He tried to pull away from the splinter, which dug into the flesh of his bare arm.

Ladybell ran at Johnny, who pushed her aside. He fired in Slocum's direction, shattering the casement. Suddenly Slocum was free. He rolled out of the window, landing on the porch roof. His momentum carried him down the angle of the roof into the cool early morning air, onto the hard ground.

Slocum lost his breath for a moment. His tight chest burned for air. He filled his lungs as Johnny Pike's weapon exploded from above.

"Run!" cried Ladybell.

Slocum reached for the reins of the pinto. Johnny's pistol kept barking. The pinto reared and then shuddered. It fell to the ground, kicking its back legs. A slug from Johnny's pistol had hit the pinto in the head. The mount wasn't going to make any getaway.

Johnny's revolver clicked empty above Slocum. "I'm comin' down for you, you bastard! I'm gonna kill you!"

Johnny's silhouette left the window frame. Ladybell shouted down to Slocum, telling him that Lin Ching would hide him in the laundry room. Slocum didn't listen to her. He just stood his ground, drawing the old Navy. When Johnny rushed out of the house, charging headlong, Slocum lifted the pistol and took aim. He squeezed off only to hear the muffled click of a misfire.

"Damn!"

He gave it another try but the Colt had jammed on him. Johnny Pike tackled Slocum and knocked him to the ground. Johnny flailed at him with clenched fists until Slocum caught him squarely on the chin with a short right hand. Johnny buckled under the jaw-shot and rolled off for a second.

Slocum scrambled to his feet, trying to cock the Navy. The cylinder wouldn't free up. He was standing there naked and unable to defend himself.

Johnny Pike had already drawn another gun from some-where inside his duster. Slocum looked into the tiny bore of a pocket revolver. Johnny had it pointed at his chest.

"You're gonna pay for hurtin' my Bell," Johnny railed. "Can't nobody treat her like a whore."

"That's what she is," Slocum replied.

He had to make a move, jump away, at least give Johnny a moving target.

"You know what I'm gonna do," Johnny said. "I'm gonna shoot your dick off, you adulterous bastard."

He lowered the weapon, aiming it at Slocum's crotch.

Johnny laughed. "Yeah, from now on, I shoot off the dick of any man who bothers my Bell."

"Gonna be a lotta dickless cowboys," Slocum droned.

Johnny closed one eye, sighting down the barrel. "Say good-bye to your pecker, you cheatin' rat."

"Not his pecker!" Ladybell cried from above.

Slocum only had one choice. He threw the Colt at Johnny Pike. The butt of the weapon hit him in the middle of his chest. Then, to Slocum's surprise, the damned pistol exploded, sending lead, burning powder, and gunmetal into Johnny's face. The pocket revolver fell from his hand. Johnny tumbled to the ground with his palms to his eyes.

As Johnny squirmed and squealed in the spring mud, Slocum grabbed the pocket revolver. He thumbed back the hammer and took aim. Ladybell screamed from behind him, begging him not to kill Johnny. Her plea was so pitiful that Slocum spared the blinded gunman.

"He was gonna shoot my dick off," Slocum said.

Ladybell knelt next to Johnny. "Thank God he's not dead."

"He should be."

She glared at Slocum. "Get your clothes on and get out of here."

Slocum pointed to the pinto. "He shot my mount."

"Take Johnny's horse."

Slocum shook his head. "He's got *compañeros* around here. If they see me on his mount, they'll know Johnny didn't give it to me."

"Just go!" Ladybell replied. "You've caused enough trouble."

"Me?"

Laughter resounded from behind Slocum. The working girls and some of their all-night customers had been awakened by the commotion. They formed an audience in the open windows of the cathouse.

Ladybell stood up and waved them back into the shadows. "Ain't nothin' here that nobody needs to see. Get back to bed. Somebody tell Lin Ching to bring bandages."

Slocum searched for his clothes, putting them on bit by bit. Everything was damp and soiled. The Chinaman had wasted his time washing them.

By the time Slocum was dressed, the Chinaman had helped Ladybell drag the wounded Johnny into the upstairs bedroom. Ladybell looked down from the window again. Slocum just shrugged at her.

Ladybell motioned to the west. "Git gone. Go back to town."

"I ain't got no mount," Slocum replied. "Your boyfriend saw to that. He owes me a horse."

"And you owe him a pair of eyes," she cried. "You blinded him."

"I need a horse, woman!"

"Walk back to town for all I care!"

She slammed the window shut.

Slocum sighed, thinking that he had gone from paradise to hell in a couple of hateful minutes. He leaned against the hitching rail for a while, looking at the dead pinto. It had been a good mount, certainly not deserving of a stray bullet from Johnny Pike's gun.

"Damned woman!"

The window went up again. "I heard that," Ladybell called. "You better get out of here fast."

"I want a horse!"

She pointed a finger at him. "You're gonna get the sheriff!"

Slocum held up his hands. "No lawmen. I hate lawmen."

"Then get your rebel ass out of here!"

"You don't have to tell me again."

The window slammed with a bang. Slocum came off the rail post. The sun was up now, illuminating the warm carcass of the pinto. Slocum figured the Chinaman would have plenty of stew meat for a while.

Slocum wrestled the pinto for the saddle, finally freeing

his tack from the dead animal. Its corpse was still twitching. Slocum gathered his belongings and hoisted them on his shoulder. He wondered how far it was back to Cheyenne. The ride hadn't seemed that long, but it was another thing to walk it with a saddle on your shoulder.

"Damned woman. A hundred dollars. Gold."

It didn't seem worth it now as he cleared the back of the house and started on the road to town. A stiff, cold wind bore down from the northwest, blowing in Slocum's face. His damp coat didn't help much, not with the wet clothing underneath it. At least the sun was rising higher.

But the sun didn't help much. Clouds weren't far behind, smothering any hope of warmth. By the time Slocum could see the shapes of Cheyenne in the distance, the sky was raining on him again, emptying wet buckets and miring the ground to impede his progress.

Dottie, the dirty blond girl who had summoned Johnny Pike, stood in the kitchen gossiping with the other whores. "You should have seen it," she said. "That cowboy come out of the window and boom, he rolled all the way to the ground. Then Johnny shot his horse and—"

"We know all about that," replied one of the other girls. "But how did Johnny find out that cowboy was with Ladybell?"

Dottie blushed. "Well, I—I don't—"

"Yes! Why don't you tell us who told Johnny!"

Ladybell stood in the doorway with her hands on her hips. "Go on, Dottie, tell us who went into town to find Johnny."

Dottie lowered her eyes to the floor. "I don't know, Ladybell. I—"

Ladybell gestured to the air. "You girls find somethin' else to do. I'm going to talk to Dottie alone."

When the others had left, Ladybell came close to Dottie, stroking her ratty hair. "You went to get Johnny, didn't you?"

"No ma'am, I—"

Ladybell grabbed her hair and yanked it hard. "You little bitch, you almost got him killed!"

"No, I swear I—"

Ladybell dragged her across the room by the hair, slamming her into the wall. "You're gonna pay for this."

"I didn't—"

"Johnny told me. Told me it was you that come and got him. He never would have come if you hadn't called him."

"Please, Miss Ladybell, don't hurt me. I didn't mean to—"

"You know what I'm gonna do?" Ladybell said. "I'm gonna save you. You're gonna be locked in your room. I'm saving you."

"Save me? How—"

"Saving you for the next cattle drive that comes through here. Them cowboys is gonna get all they want for one dollar. You been wantin' to whore, now you got your chance."

"Ladybell, no, I—"

"I won't make any money, but you'll be happy!"

"No, please—"

The girl's cries could be heard above the pouring rain. Ladybell dragged her to the back of the place, locking her in a small room. Dottie had brought it on herself, the madam thought. Now she had to lie in the bed she had made.

Nobody seemed to notice Slocum's wary trek up the muddy street. Cheyenne was hiding from the rain. Even the windows of the sheriff's office were fogged and dark. Slocum hoped he could get to the stable without being seen by the lawman. Maybe the stableman would give him a break for a couple of days. He had to get a mount if he was ever going to leave Wyoming.

Lights burned in the saloon, but Slocum didn't have the price of a drink. Ladybell had fed him too much of her sweet liquor, leaving him with a headache. Some hair of the dog would have tasted good. He just kept moving in the direction of the livery.

As he drew nearer the stables, Slocum saw that a stagecoach was parked in front of the barn doors. He hesitated for a moment, wondering if this might have something to do with the law. But then he remembered the stableman telling him that the stage stopped at the livery twice a week.

Slocum trudged on, entering the livery through a side door. There were two stage men talking to the stableman. They all turned to look at Slocum when he entered. Slocum nodded and dropped his saddle. They didn't appear threatening.

The stableman smiled. "Hey, John. You're back. I was just tellin' these two boys about you."

Slocum's hand dropped beside the butt of the pocket revolver that was wedged in his belt. "Me?"

A rough-looking man pushed back his hat and sized up Slocum. "Well, he's big enough. Can you use a gun, mister?"

Slocum eyed the stranger. "Who wants to know?"

The man took off his hat. "Sorry, I'm Jess Carpenter, driver of that stage out there. This is Shorty, my shotgun rider."

Slocum nodded. "What you want with me?"

"Need an extra shotgun rider on the run to Rock Springs," Carpenter replied. "You lookin' for work?"

Slocum lowered his gun hand. "I am. You're plannin' to take that stage to Rock Springs in this rain?"

Shorty laughed. "Got to, sonny. It's our job."

"My name ain't sonny," Slocum replied. "Call me John."

Carpenter held out a double-barreled shotgun. "Don't care much what they call you, sir. If you can handle this, you've got a ride to Rock Springs and fifty dollars in gold when we get there."

Slocum could hardly believe the change in luck. He had walked right into an escape route. Still, some things had to be considered before he said yes. Riding shotgun on a stage was dangerously close to being a lawman, something Slocum swore he would never do. He also had to wonder how the stage would fare in the rain.

"How long I got to study on it?" Slocum asked.

"Until them horses are changed," Carpenter replied.

He was a confounded old cuss with a white beard that hid his face and a wet hat that hid his eyes. Shorty was younger, but he didn't look to be that tough. Maybe these boys did need some help. That meant they were carrying something valuable. What if they had to face bushwhackers along the trail?

On the other side, what was there to staying in Cheyenne? He was broke, mountless, and waterlogged. And pretty soon Johnny Pike's men would be looking for the *hombre* that blinded their leader.

Slocum also hated riding coaches. It was right next to train travel for the most loathsome way to traverse long distances. Bouncing up and down, the deafening rattle of the wheels and harnesses. There was always enough dust and sweat to make adobe bricks.

Where had the driver said they were going? Rock Springs. That was west. Slocum could not remember if he had ever been in Rock Springs. Maybe there weren't any posters on him there.

"What do you say, John?" the driver asked. "Are you going to ride out with us? We'll be ready to go in a few minutes."

"I'll need those minutes," Slocum replied.

The stableman moved closer to Slocum. "Hey, they're good men. If they say they'll pay you, they will."

Slocum had to try his last option. "I was wonderin' if there was any work I could do in trade for a mount?"

The stableman shook his head. "Partner, I can't afford to give up a red penny. I'm barely makin' it as it is."

Slocum picked up his wet gear. "Then it looks like I'm ridin' the stage."

He brushed past the stableman, heading for the driver.

"Hey, aren't you gonna thank me for gettin' you this job?"

Slocum just kept walking. He hadn't chosen the job. The job had chosen him. He was leaving one trouble for another. The only thing he could be sure of was the trouble he was running *from*.

He took the double-barrel from the driver. "It loaded?"

Carpenter nodded. "Hair triggers, so don't cock them hammers unless you mean business."

Slocum hesitated in the barn door, looking up at the strongbox that rested behind the driver's seat. The box was the future trouble. Trouble had the good hand, and Slocum had to bet on a pair of hair triggers.

4

The stage journey had been uneventful so far, but that didn't make Slocum hate it any less. He had been bounced and jostled in the hard leather seat, which made his insides feel like they had been beaten with a short stick. His tailbone ached, his legs were sore, and his gut churned with the sickness that came with riding too fast on bumpy roads.

Surprisingly, the spring rains had not been a problem. The trail seemed to be holding up well enough to keep the coach moving. Only once had the wheels become mired in the road, forcing everyone to get out and push. Slocum didn't like it very much, but he had to endure if he was going to see the fifty dollars at the end of the trip. Some men would have looked on it as easy money. However, Slocum would have traded the miserable ride and the twin-barreled scatter-gun for anything, including a mule skinner's job.

The other passengers hadn't made things any easier.

Riding inside the compartment were a tall, red-haired man, his pretty new wife, and a young army officer. The blue-belly soldier made Slocum nervous enough, but the red-haired man was a law officer who was traveling to Rock Springs to assume the sheriff's job there. His bride was a blond girl with roving blue eyes that had played furtively with Slocum's own gaze along the way. The tall man from Georgia just kept quiet, as did the other riders until they picked up the whiskey drummer in Elk Mountain.

The drummer was a twitchy, nosy, weasel-faced man who immediately inquired as to the names and histories of the other passengers. Slocum naturally ignored him, but the others gave up information without hesitation. The sheriff's name was Brick Hanson and he was a former policeman from Kansas City who had come west to make a name for himself as a sheriff. His wife's name was Addie and though she acted sweet enough, Slocum thought she had a certain worn edge to her, a frayed quality that he had seen in women who were not usually married to lawmen. The cavalry officer was a young lieutenant named Arthur Rabon and he had official army business in Rock Springs, though he would not divulge the nature of his mission. Slocum suspected that the officer had something to do with the strongbox that rode above them on top of the coach.

From Elk Mountain to the narrow passes of the Great Divide, the drummer kept talking, which brought out the jaw-flapping natures of the sheriff and the soldier. Hanson was particularly willing to offer his views on how to handle outlaws, namely to deposit them at the end of a short rope. The soldier agreed wholeheartedly that hanging was a fitting end for any criminal or renegade, no matter how small the offense.

The drummer helped to lubricate the conversation by offering samples of the whiskey he was peddling. The sheriff and the soldier both took small nips. Addie, the lawman's wife, declined, but Slocum thought she had that look in her eye, the hankering glint that told Slocum she really wanted to take a nip with the rest of the gang.

But Slocum managed to stop listening to them after a while. He just rode the damnable seat, keeping the shotgun on his lap. Outside the coach window, the landscape flew by his green eyes, promising an eventual end to the journey. He had it all planned out in his mind—get the fifty dollars, buy a horse, and head south to the warmth of New Mexico or Arizona. To hell with coaches and lawmen and loud-mouthed drummers. Slocum wanted to be in the saddle again, guiding his mount at a pace more suited to a drifter. A pace that he would not know for quite some time.

The coach ground to a halt that woke Slocum with the screeching whinny of the horses. He roused from his nap, as did the other passengers. They looked out the windows to see the spring sun beating down on the high walls of a mountain pass. Slocum put his thumb on the shotgun hammers when he heard the driver dropping down out of the upper seat.

The door flung open. "Y'all can take a stretch if you've a mind to," the driver said. "Shorty and I gotta study on this river."

Slocum stepped out, gazing toward the swollen waters of the stream that rushed forward with white froth. It didn't look too deep, but high water could be deceiving, especially to coach wheels. He sighed dejectedly, thinking that the trip had gone too smoothly. He wondered if the river would be their undoing.

Shorty was slipping a feed bag on the horses. "Thayer's on the other side," he said to Slocum. "We can give these animals a blow and then change up the road. Won't be far to Rock Springs from there."

Slocum nodded absently, searching the high slopes for signs of movement. The mountain passes presented too many places for bushwhackers to hide. He figured if an ambush was coming, it would be soon, between the river and Rock Springs. They wouldn't be out of danger until they were at the stage stop in town. Anything could happen in the meantime.

The young soldier came up beside him, studying the rapid waters. "Could this mean a delay?"

"Maybe," Slocum replied.

Shorty laughed. "No need for y'all to be so long-faced. We've crossed this creek more'n once in worse conditions. Carpenter just wants to check it to make sure there ain't no surprises since the last time."

The sheriff was right there with his wife. "Doesn't look that bad to me," he offered. "I've seen worse."

Mrs. Hanson was leaning against the coach, scrutinizing her face in a small mirror. "I wouldn't know anything about such things," she said. "I just want this journey to be finished."

Shorty squinted toward the coach. "Where's that drummer? We could all use a snort about now."

The weasel-faced liquor salesman stepped out of the compartment. "Fret not, sir. I have what we are all in need of."

From the corner of his eye, Slocum saw the woman lick her lips. The drummer passed the bottle around until she was the only one left who had not drunk. She flinched when the drummer started to put the bottle away.

"Sir," she said quickly, "if you don't mind—"

Sheriff Hanson turned to glare at her. "Addie!"

She grabbed the left side of her face. "A terrible toothache has come on me, Brick. I don't want to drink, mind you, but I thought a little dab on my tooth might help."

Hanson frowned dubiously, but he gave in to her feminine deception. "Oh, all right, but don't take a lot. You aren't used to it."

Addie smiled weakly. "Oh, I won't, Brick. I promise."

The men all turned their gaze to the driver, who was still wading across the rolling stream. Slocum watched sidelong as Addie lifted the bottle and took a healthy slug. She knew liquor all right. Slocum had to wonder what other secrets she was keeping.

In her blue dress, she resembled a Quaker woman with a bonnet to cover her flaxen hair. The buxom curves had been subdued beneath the dress, but they were still there. Slocum still thought she was a mite loose in her manners, though he could not figure out why she would marry a lawman or why a lawman would be interested in her.

It didn't matter because the driver was wading out of the river. "She's not too bad."

Shorty squinted at him. "Think we ought to try it?"

Carpenter nodded. "I want me a slug of that firewater before we do it, though. Need to fortify myself."

Addie, who was still holding the bottle, looked embarrassed. "Oh, here, take it."

Carpenter frowned at her. "Yes'm, thank you."

"She has a toothache," her husband insisted.

"Fine by me," Carpenter replied, lifting the bottle to his lips.

Shorty also drank and then appealed to the driver. "We got to spell these horses," he said. "I got 'em feedin' and then they'll want to drink."

Carpenter gazed toward the sky. "Still plenty of daylight left. I could use a nap myself."

Slocum nodded to the west. "I thought we were just a stone's throw from Thayer."

"We are," Carpenter replied. "What's the matter?"

The tall man from Georgia turned his eyes to the high slopes. "Nothin'. I'll just feel better when we're out of these passes."

Carpenter laughed nervously. "So will I, pardner. So will I."

Lieutenant Rabon also lifted his eyes to the peaks. "Are you saying that we've got cause to be worried?"

Slocum pointed to the strongbox. "Till we deliver that to Rock Springs, we got plenty of reason to worry."

Addie shuddered, prompting her husband to slide a reassuring arm around her shoulders. "Don't worry, honey. We've all got guns."

Carpenter stroked his mustache, gazing ahead on the trail. "Maybe the Reb has got something. I guess we could keep moving."

"What about the animals?" Shorty asked. "I fed 'em and now they want to drink. They might get sick if we—"

Carpenter shook his head. "I'll walk 'em slow. How's that sound, Reb?"

Slocum shrugged. "I ain't in charge here."

"No," Carpenter replied. "But I am. So I say, we cross this stream and keep on keepin' on. We can rest when we get to Thayer."

The drummer's face had turned white. "I go along with the Reb. Who knows what's waitin' in here? Could be thieves or Indians."

Rabon laughed. "I can assure you, sir, that there are no hostile redskins between here and Rock Springs."

Carpenter started to climb up into the driver's seat. "Maybe not, but it might serve us to ride on while we got clear skies."

All of them were in agreement, even Shorty. When the coach was full again, Carpenter shook the reins and the coach began to roll over the rocky streambed. They held their breaths in midstream, feeling each stone and hole in the river. For a moment, it seemed that the current might get the better of the coach. The rushing waters rose enough to spill through the cracks in the stage doors.

But Carpenter managed to get the team to pull them onto the opposite bank. They came out of the water a little wetter, but safe and sound. Carpenter urged the horses along the dry trail, keeping a slow but steady pace for the next stop on the run.

Slocum and the other men kept their eyes trained out of the window, watching the shadows that seemed to move in and out of the rocks above them. But there was no attack from the cliffs. The stage rolled into Thayer around dusk, stopping in front of a little stone house that smelled of fresh stew.

The team was unhitched and the passengers quickly settled into the house where they were fed dinner by a smiling man named Smitty. Encouraged by everyone, including the lady with the mock toothache, the drummer poured shots of redeye after the meal. Smitty stoked a fire that warmed the little enclosure, making everyone feel comfortable. Everyone but Slocum. He just wanted the damned trek to be over.

Carpenter, who had chosen to drink coffee instead of hooch, called Slocum outside after a while. They moved toward the coach in the evening shadows. Carpenter wanted to be out of earshot of the others when he spoke to the tall man from Georgia.

"I want to move on tonight," Carpenter said. "Give the rest another few minutes by the fire and then head out. What do you think?"

Slocum sighed. "I ain't sure. Why you want to move now?"

"You know why," the driver replied.

Slocum nodded toward the roof of the coach. "The strongbox. Right?"

"Sure enough," Carpenter said. "See, we always stop here overnight. But I got a feelin' it'd be better to go now. I know the trail and I don't mind drivin' at night. I ain't never been held up in the dark, so it's kinda like a superstition with me."

"Yeah?"

"You don't say much, Reb."

"I'm listenin', Carpenter. And you're makin' a lot of sense."

The driver sighed. "Well, I been around these parts a while. Ain't no sense in stickin' a hand at a snake unless you aim to let him bite you. I'm all for pushin' on. Course, the others may not like it."

"Who cares what they like?"

Slocum just wanted to be closer to a warm bed and his fifty dollars.

"You want to tell 'em?" Carpenter asked.

"No."

The driver started to turn toward the stone house. "You're right, it's my job. Reckon I better—"

"Carpenter!"

He turned back to face Slocum. "Yep?"

"If we leave tonight, how long before we're in Rock Springs?"

"Noon at the latest, pro'bly mornin'."

Slocum looked to the west. "Daylight?"

"No, pro'bly after, but not much after. Not if the trail is clear and we don't have any—"

Slocum raised his hand. "Don't say it."

Carpenter laughed. "You got your superstitions too." He walked off to tell the passengers to get ready to travel.

Slocum kept his green eyes trained on the dark trail to the west. A lot of men felt that it was better not to talk of trouble. Others thought if you said something beforehand, anticipating trouble, that it wouldn't happen. Slocum was one of the men who thought it best not to speak of trouble. He just wanted to get through the last leg of the journey with the ease that had preceded them.

He stayed by the coach until he heard someone moving behind him. His hand reached down to the pocket revolver he had taken from Johnny Pike. But then he smelled the perfume on the cool night air and he knew that the woman had come out of the stone house.

"Well," she said half-accusingly, "I guess it's your fault that we're going on tonight instead of sleeping."

"Ain't nothin' my fault," Slocum replied. "Carpenter thinks we're better off if we leave tonight."

She sighed in an obvious way, but when Slocum did not respond, she moved closer, brushing against him. "Where do you hail from, cowboy?"

The question came out too casual, like she had asked it a hundred times before. Slocum kept his mouth shut. He didn't take to sparking another man's wife, not when the man was a few yards away with a big six-shooter in his holster. Hanson carried a Peacemaker and he probably knew how to use it.

Of course, ignoring a woman didn't necessarily mean that she would stop talking to you. Sometimes it meant the opposite. Ignoring her gave her more room to flap her lips.

"What kind of town is Rock Springs?" she asked.

Slocum shrugged. "Don't know. Never been there."

"Is it a dangerous town?"

"I told ya, I don't know."

She sighed, but not like she was worried. The question had been blank. If she was fretting about her husband's dangerous line of work, she didn't seem to be showing her fears.

"Brick and I got married when he found his new job," she went on. "I'm glad he took it. I—"

"Addie! Are you out here?"

Sheriff Hanson had appeared in the doorway of the stone house. He wasn't really a bad man, even if he did have a badge waiting for him in Rock Springs. Slocum might have liked him in another situation. It was just that the tall rebel didn't much like any kind of lawman, especially one with a flirty wife.

"I'm out here," Addie replied in a bored tone. "This gentleman was just assuring me that we aren't in any danger."

Hanson came out to put his arm around his wife's waist. "That's mighty kind of you, sir. I happen to agree that we should move on tonight. I reckon my little wife here would like to sleep a spell, but it makes sense to push forward. Wouldn't you say so?"

Slocum just nodded as the sheriff drew his wife closer to him. Their stage ride was almost over. But Slocum figured Hanson was the one with the rough trip ahead. Little Miss Addie appeared to be a whole lot of bumpy road. Slocum wanted to get the hell away from both of them.

"All them that's comin', come on," Carpenter called.

They loaded up again and started for Rock Springs, rolling along under a dark, moonless sky on a night that was tailor-made for ambushers.

5

Slocum dreamed restlessly of Ladybell. She was rocking back and forth in bed, extending her arms to him, begging him to join her. He began to stretch out next to her but Johnny Pike stopped him again, just the way it had happened at the Cheyenne cathouse. The memory of the concussive thud of lightning gunshots startled him awake in the belly of the coach.

The familiar rattle of the carriage greeted the big man from Georgia. He wiped his eyes. The coach hit a bump and the window covering flapped open a bit to let a streak of sunlight inside the compartment. Slocum's eyes grew wider at the promise of daybreak. If the sun was already up, then they couldn't be far from Rock Springs and the end of the hellish journey.

" 'Bout damned time," he muttered to himself, shifting the scatter-gun that had grown heavy on his lap.

Slocum just wanted the trip to be finished. There hadn't been any trouble—a turn of luck in his favor. Still, he knew that anything could happen as long as they were in transit with the strongbox. They weren't in Rock Springs yet.

Lifting his hand, he drew back the leather shade that covered the window. The sun glinted on moist faces of rock walls above the hurtling vehicle. They were going through another pass. Suddenly everything seemed familiar to Slocum. Had he been this way before? His ramblings might have taken him to western Wyoming, although there were a hundred or a thousand places in the Rockies that looked the same.

Closing the flap, he turned his eyes back to the other passengers. He looked at the woman first. Addie was asleep on her husband's shoulder. Slocum had seen the face before. Not the exact countenance, but similar faces in cathouses and saloons. The pretty jaw was now slack, mouth hanging open, the red rouge smudged beyond recognition. He had woken up next to her or at least a bunch of women who were just like her.

The husband, Sheriff Brick Hanson, dozed calmly with his head back and his Stetson over his eyes. He was a rock of a man. Probably read the Bible every morning before he went off to work. Hanson had taken a shot of whiskey along the way, but that still wasn't enough to make Slocum actually like him. Then again, Slocum didn't like much of anybody, which was the main reason he had become a drifter and a saddle tramp.

Slocum felt a sudden pressure on his shoulder. The whiskey drummer had leaned over on him. Slocum pushed the weasel back against the wall of the carriage interior. Slocum didn't care much for the drummer, even though the redeye salesman had kept them all lubricated for the ride. Slocum wouldn't have admitted it to anyone, but he was glad that the salesman had brought samples with him. The hooch had made everything a lot easier.

The carriage thundered on toward Rock Springs. Carpenter yelled at the team from the driver's seat. Slocum could barely hear his voice over the noise of the wheels. He thought he might go deaf from the din.

Leaning back on the seat, Slocum embraced the scatter-gun and reflected on his plight. Things weren't so bad now, not as bad as they had been in Cheyenne. He had escaped the trouble. Of course, he had lost his mount, but there was fifty dollars waiting for him at the end of the line. That fifty would go a long way toward buying a nag or a mule. He might even have a couple of dollars left over for a meal and a bottle of rotgut. With a full belly and some whiskey to fortify him, it wouldn't take Slocum long to get the hell out of Wyoming.

Across the seat from him, the young lieutenant awoke with a start. The blue-belly officer yawned and stretched. He turned his gaze on Slocum, smiling at the tall man. Slocum didn't even nod. He just looked away, filled with revulsion at the sight of a soldier in a Union uniform.

The lieutenant glanced at the other passengers. "Sleeping like babies," he said to Slocum. "Amazing how anyone can sleep on such a bumpy ride."

Slocum lifted the shade again, peering into the morning light. The walls of rock still flanked the coach. They had to be close to Rock Springs. Carpenter had promised an early arrival.

"You don't like soldiers much, do you, sir?" the young lieutenant asked.

Slocum ignored him, keeping his green eyes on the trail.

"I take it you fought for the Confederacy," the lieutenant went on. "I don't blame you for being bitter, sir. But I can assure you that I feel no animosity at all toward any son of Dixie. Now that the war is over—"

"The war ain't over," Slocum snapped, not looking at the blue-belly. "It ain't never gonna be over."

"That's hardly a good way of looking at it, sir. I—"

Slocum pointed a finger at him. "You blue bellies killed off everythin'. You ain't got no rebels to kill anymore, so you done it to the Injuns."

The blue belly stiffened indignantly. "I'll have you know, sir, that we are here to protect the God-fearing men and women who have chosen to settle these accursed territories. Subduing the savages was a natural turn of—"

"Shut up," Slocum said. "You ain't in charge of me."

He looked out the window again. The coach burst into a clearing that shimmered with bright light. They had run up on an opening in the sheer walls of stone. Slocum thought he saw puffs of mist on the rocky crags of a low ridge. The morning fog hadn't burned off yet.

A dull thump seemed to rise up out of the coach. But they hadn't hit a rock or a chug hole. The ride seemed smoother than ever. Then there was a tap on the shade of the window next to the lieutenant.

Slocum gazed toward the soldier whose head had snapped back against the seat. Slocum thought the blue belly was going to give him more grief, but the lieutenant only smiled in a sick way. His head began to roll around on his neck, like it was too heavy to support.

Slocum grimaced at the man. "You all right?"

The lieutenant opened his mouth to speak but no sounds came out of his maw. His head lolled back again. He reached for his throat, where his kerchief was tied in a knot.

A smear of crimson appeared at the knot. Suddenly the lieutenant began to tear at the kerchief. When he ripped it away, Slocum saw the hole in his throat. Blood gushed out of the opening.

"What the . . . ?"

Slocum heard the gunshots. They sounded like firecrackers against the noise of the carriage. The shade flicked again. A second bullet tore through the lieutenant's face.

"Son of a bitch!"

The soldier fell forward, twitching as the life flowed from his body. Slocum opened the door and quickly pushed him out. There was no need to have a corpse in the way if they were going to fight ambushers.

"Hanson! Wake up!"

The would-be sheriff opened his eyes. "What—"

"Bushwhackers," Slocum replied. "Draw that Peacemaker if you know how to use it."

Hanson frowned. "I don't hear any—"

Somewhere a rifle exploded, sending lead through the compartment. Slocum looked over at the whiskey drummer. The man's eyes were open but he was not awake. Blood poured from a hole in his chest.

Hanson lifted the Colt from its holster. "Where are they?"

"How the hell should I know?" Slocum replied.

He pushed the drummer out of the coach. Hanson frowned at him. But Slocum didn't have time to jaw with the lawman.

"Carpenter," the tall man muttered.

He could hear the muffled shouts of the driver. Shorty's own scatter-gun erupted, but there was no chance of the shot hitting anything. The ambushers were probably hiding in the low rocks. And from the sound of the rifle fire, there had to be a lot of them.

Hanson drew back the shade, gazing toward the ridge. "I don't see them. Maybe I can get off a shot."

"No!" Slocum cried. "Wait. We might run out of this. Just keep that hog leg ready."

Mrs. Hanson raised her head. "What is it?"

Hanson pushed her down into his lap. "Stay calm, honey. Everything is going to be all right."

"I doubt it," Slocum muttered.

Hanson glared at Slocum. "Don't talk to her like that. There's no need to scare her."

"You'd be scared too, if you wasn't a brainless lawman," Slocum replied.

Hanson blustered until another slug cut through the stage. The sheriff held his wife tightly, lowering his own head. Getting ambushed was a lot different from rousting drunks and cowboys in a Kansas City saloon.

Slocum had to get to Carpenter. He had to know what was ahead on the trail. Surely the bushwhackers didn't hope to take the stage just by firing on them. There had to be another angle, some riders ahead on the road or some kind of barricade.

"Carpenter!" Slocum cried.

The stage's rattling was the only reply. The driver and the shotgun man couldn't hear him. What good would it do anyway if they could hear him? Slocum didn't have the slightest clue about how to get out of the ambush.

Carpenter just kept them moving, bouncing on the road. The rifles stopped for a moment. Had they outrun the gunfire?

"We're clear," Hanson said.

He started to lift the shade away from the window.

"Don't!" Slocum hollered.

But Hanson pulled back the covering. Shots rang out again. Someone screeched in the driver's seat. Shorty fell from his perch, tumbling back to grab the rim of the window.

Hanson stared into the bloody face. "My God!"

Slocum reached for Shorty, but the shotgun rider lost his grip and fell away to be crushed under the iron-rimmed wheel. Shorty was gone. The driver had to be next.

"Carpenter!" Slocum bellowed again.

What good was it to holler? They were going to be finished if the stage didn't make it through the line of fire. Slocum knew he couldn't do much, but he wanted to do more than hang on for his life.

"I can't stand this!" Hanson cried.

Peeling back the shade, the lawman emptied his Peacemaker into thin air. Nobody was hit on the ridge. All the shooting accomplished was to fill the compartment with smoke. Slocum gagged on the stench of burnt powder.

"Hanson, you idiot!"

"Do something!"

Slocum just shook his head. Some lawman. The citizens of Rock Springs weren't going to be much safer when Hanson arrived. *If* Hanson arrived.

"Carpenter!"

He had to take a look out the window. Slocum drew a deep breath and then lifted the shade. He stuck his head through the opening, craning his neck to get a look at the driver.

Carpenter was hunched down in the seat, trying to control the reins of the team as the guns blazed above him. They were shooting from both sides of the road, wanting to catch the stage in their cross fire.

"Carpenter!"

The driver did not reply, but something came flying out of the seat. Slocum caught the object in his left hand. When he had ducked back into the compartment, he saw that Carpenter had thrown him a rifle.

"What's that?" Hanson asked desperately.

"A Winchester," Slocum replied, levering a cartridge into the chamber. "Better than that damned scatter-gun."

Hanson tried to reach across the compartment. "Give me that weapon."

Slocum pointed the bore at Hanson's chest. "Back off, lawman. I ain't gonna let you get me killed."

The woman began to shriek. "Leave him alone!"

"Shut up, whore!" Slocum cried.

Hanson's face contorted from fear to rage. "I won't allow you to talk to my wife like that!"

But Slocum couldn't hear him. He had to take a shot with the Winchester. It might not do any good to fire into the hills, but it could sure as hell make him feel better. At least he wouldn't go down without a fight.

Slocum hung out the window again, aiming the Winchester at nothing. He squeezed off a round in the direction of some rocks ahead of him. It felt so good that he let go with another volley.

"The river!" he heard Carpenter cry. "The river, cowboy!"

Slocum drew back into the compartment. Why the hell was Carpenter hollering about a river? Unless—they were going to crash headlong into a stream. And Carpenter knew it. The ambushers knew it too.

"Bastards!"

Did Carpenter have something planned or was he just afraid? What else could he do but run headlong into the water? Unless he planned to turn around. An about-face would take them right back into the line of fire.

Hanson reached for the rifle again. Slocum let him take it. One Winchester wasn't going to do any good, not from the compartment of the coach. The bushwhackers could keep them pinned all day if they didn't clear the rocks. How much farther was it to town anyway?

Hanson levered the rifle. "I'm going to give them a little taste of their own medicine!" He put the barrel through the window and let go until the weapon was empty.

"You're wastin' bullets!" Slocum cried.

Hanson started to say something, but he never got the chance. Several slugs ripped through the windows, tearing into his body. Blood began to pour from his chest and stomach.

The horror of becoming a widow spread over the face of the woman. "Brick! No!"

Hanson started to writhe in agony. He was hit bad. But Slocum couldn't help the lawman, not with the shower of lead raining down on them.

The woman fell across the seat, grabbing at Slocum's legs. "Do something! Don't let him die."

Slocum pushed her back. "That's outta my hands."

She sobbed as the blood oozed all over her husband's fine suit.

Slocum reloaded the Winchester. He leaned out the window, firing at nothing and everything. He could not see the river yet. It had to be up around the rocky bend.

"Carpenter!"

More shots came from above, splintering the wooden panels around him. Slocum did not retreat. He pulled the trigger of the Winchester but there was no report from the barrel. He had emptied it.

"Carpenter!"

He looked up toward the driver's seat. Carpenter's face appeared suddenly against the morning sky. He thought the mustached man was going to throw him another weapon, but

Carpenter only grabbed his chest and fell away from the stage. His body tumbled onto the road.

"Damn!"

As soon as Carpenter let go of the reins, the team began to slow. Muzzle bursts echoed all around them. If the horses didn't speed up, he was going to be peppered to death with rifle slugs.

Slocum had to get to the driver's seat. It was his only chance to make the team run hard again. He heard the woman crying behind him as he pulled his body through the opening. The carriage rattled and shook as he tried to wriggle his way on top of the vehicle.

He had to make it. It didn't matter that bullets were shattering the roof of the coach. He crawled toward the reins which were only inches ahead. His fingers brushed the fresh blood that had belonged to the driver and the shotgun rider. It would be his own blood if he didn't get the team moving.

He saw the reins bouncing on the seat. The leather thongs looked like snakes in a ball. His hand reached out. He could almost feel the rawhide in his grip.

"Got 'em!"

Slocum clutched the reins in his right hand. But it didn't matter. He never got a chance to hurry the team. The coach had turned the bend and was now heading straight for the river.

He tried to stop the team, but it was too late. The coach hit the river and flipped like a toy wagon in a flash flood. Slocum flew into the air, sailing headlong into the frothy chop of the swollen stream. When he landed, the darkness came over him in a hateful rush.

6

Slocum felt the wet rocks against his face before he opened his green eyes. He lay still for a moment, trying to muster his strength. His whole body was cold and aching. The unwanted dip in the stream had left him waterlogged. He could hear the cursed babbling behind him.

Slocum sat up quickly. His head spun with pain and confusion. He touched the sore spot on top of his head. There didn't seem to be any blood. No gashes either. The water had broken his fall.

Reaching for the bank, he steadied himself on the rocks. Apparently he had been washed up on the shore. He was lucky that he hadn't drowned in the frothing river. What the hell was the name of the river anyway? And where the hell was he?

Turning his eyes toward the clear blue sky, he studied the sun which still hung low over the ridge in the distance. It was morning. The sun wasn't high enough for anything else. Where had he been this morning?

"Wyoming," he said to himself in a whisper.

He had been in Cheyenne. Running from trouble there. Then he was on a stagecoach. He had been heading for . . .

"Rock Springs!"

The stage had been caught in an ambush. Slocum remembered grabbing for the reins but he did not recall flying through the air. It had happened so quickly.

"Shotgun rider."

Had he really been riding shotgun on the stage? Yes, he had done it to escape from Cheyenne. Fifty dollars at the end of the trail. Only the bushwhackers had cheated him out of the money.

"Bastards."

Lifting himself from the ground, Slocum stood on wobbly legs, peering in both directions. He could not see any signs of life. The current must have washed him downstream. But how far? And where were the bushwhackers? Had he been out for a couple of hours or a whole day? Why hadn't they found him and killed him?

Slocum had to know and the only way to do that was follow the stream in one direction or another. Maybe the river ran directly into Rock Springs. Or maybe it was just a flood water brought on by the spring runoff from the rains.

Reflexively, the tall man's hand went to his belt, searching for a weapon. He remembered the pocket revolver he had taken from Johnny Pike in Cheyenne. But the small weapon was gone. Slocum had nothing to use in self-defense, not even a rusty pocket knife.

"Damn it all."

But he knew cussing wouldn't do any good, so he turned in a circle, surveying the area around him. A high wall of rock lay to the south on the other side of the stream. A flat stretch of ground spread northward, ending at a continuance of the ridge where the bushwhackers had been hiding.

Slocum squinted back toward the east, into the current of the stream. What if the ambush party was still there, picking the bones of the stage? He sure as hell didn't want to walk up on them unarmed. The road had taken a north-south route through the rocks, which meant that the town lay downstream, west, away from the sun. It made sense to continue on in the same direction that the current had taken him. Walk the hell away from trouble, not back into another fight.

"Son of a bitchin' bastards."

The bushwhackers had ruined everything for him. What was he going to say when he walked into Rock Springs? A drifter with no gear, on foot, would attract a few eyes, especially the steely gaze of any lawmen.

But there weren't any lawmen in Rock Springs! Slocum remembered the red-haired man on the stage, Hanson was his

name. He was going to be the new sheriff of the town, but a
rifle bullet had cut short his career.

No lawmen. That was something in Slocum's favor. Maybe
he could find work there. He'd do almost anything for a meal.
Shovel shit, wrangle, sweep floors. He knew there was one
job opening—that of sheriff. He shivered at the thought. No
amount of money could make him put on a tin star.

He gazed westward, along the bank of the river. "Better get
movin'."

Slocum started walking slowly, trying to maintain his balance. His head was aching, although he had survived worse
blows to the noggin. A shot of whiskey would have helped
some. He remembered the drummer who had been killed in
the stagecoach robbery. What would he tell the town powers-
that-be about the ambush? Nothing, he decided. Let them find
out for themselves.

He followed the bend in the stream until he heard the noise
ahead of him. Slocum stopped dead in his tracks. Had he really
heard the sound of horses on the breeze? There it was again,
the unmistakable neighing of more than one mount. Where the
hell were they hiding?

He listened for the pounding of hooves but there was only
the low whinny of impatient animals. They weren't coming
toward him, which meant that they were stopped somewhere
ahead. Maybe it was the same gang that had robbed the stage.
Slocum wasn't ready to tangle with them. He ran quickly for
some boulders that formed a mound along the stream bank.

Hunkering low out of sight, Slocum kept listening for the
horses. They didn't seem to be getting any closer. He lifted
his head for a moment, peering toward the wall of rock. He
saw a man dart out into the light. The man gazed upstream,
no doubt looking for his cronies.

Slocum ducked down, hoping he had not been seen. He
figured the man had been left to watch the horses for the gang
while they shot up the stage. The bushwhackers were still picking the bones. Slocum hadn't been unconscious very long.

A burning spread through the tall man's chest. His mouth
watered for vengeance. They had it coming to them. But how
was he going to exact revenge without a weapon?

Gazing over the rocks again, he saw the man go in and out.
The lookout was becoming impatient. If Slocum could get him

by surprise, he might have a chance to at least steal one of the horses and get away before the others discovered what he had done.

It was a long shot. Too damned long. But what choice did he have? He couldn't just lay there like a stunned possum, waiting for them to ride off with everything.

Raising his head again, he gazed toward the bend where the man was hiding with the horses. What if there was more than one of them? It made sense that the rest of the gang had been on the trail, raining down lead on the stage. It would only take one man to guard the horses, Slocum told himself. He had one man between him and revenge.

The sentry stuck his head out again. He was waiting for the payoff. He had the glint of strongbox gold in his eyes. Slocum figured to give him something entirely different.

As soon as the lookout's head popped back behind the rock, Slocum started to move. He slid into the stream, paddling belly down in the current, propelling himself toward the opposite bank. The timing had to be perfect. If he caught the man by surprise, it wouldn't matter how many weapons he had on him.

The rushing water moved him swiftly toward his target. Slocum kept his eyes open. He saw the sentry's head again. The man had spotted Slocum's body in the water. Slocum took a deep breath and lowered his face into the river, spreading his arms and legs like a dead catfish. He kicked his feet a little to make sure he washed up on the opposite bank.

As he drew closer, he felt the rocks beneath his fingers. Then he heard the man's voice. He saw the shadow falling over him.

"What the hell?" the man said. "Where did—aw, he's one of the riders on that stage. Yeah, they done it good."

Slocum hesitated, holding his breath, thinking that his lungs were going to explode. He wondered if the bushwhacker was going to take the bait. Then he felt the hand on his back. The man had finally bent over him.

"Better pull you out, make sure you ain't got nothin' in your pockets. Yeah, them other boys musta—argh—"

Slocum reached up quickly, grabbing the man's neck. He squeezed for dear life, closing off the man's windpipe, choking the air out of his body. The man started to grapple with

Slocum, but it was too late. Slocum pulled him into the river, holding his head under the water.

"There you go, you bastard," Slocum said through clenched teeth. "How's it feel to be on the other end?"

The man trembled and then went limp. Slocum held him down for a few more minutes, making sure he was dead. Then he dragged the man and himself out of the stream. He looked down at the body. The man was wearing a new duster and a clean Stetson. His jeans were also fresh. He sure as hell didn't look like a desperado. Where had he come from?

Slocum reached for the man's sidearm. It was a shiny Colt Peacemaker. The metal was well-oiled, rust-free, like it had never been fired. Slocum cocked the weapon and spun in the direction of the horses, making sure that the sentry was alone. He counted eight animals in all. That left seven bushwhackers at the wreck of the stage.

Seven to one, not exactly good odds. Slocum knew he should ride on. But he was angry, as furious as an ornery renegade.

"They got it comin'," he said to himself.

But how would he do it? He only had the Peacemaker and eight horses. He searched the sling rings on the saddles, but they were empty. The ambushers had taken their rifles to pepper the stage. There was only one Winchester in the scabbard of the sentry's horse.

"One rifle, one pistol."

What if he did take one of the horses and ride into town? Would he be mistaken for a member of the gang? Of course, he could steer around Rock Springs, but that wouldn't mean much if they sent out a posse after the gang. He could even be caught by the men who had robbed the stage.

"Better to face it now," he told himself.

He looked down at the body of the drowned man. They were close to the same size. Maybe he could pull it off. He had the horses. The plan had already begun to form in his mind. And in his anger, Slocum told himself that it would work.

The leader of the gang was a tall, scarfaced man called Tarkey. He stood with a rifle on his hip, watching as the other six men rummaged through the remains of the stagecoach. They already had the strongbox resting safely on the bank of the stream. Now they were swarming over the carcass like a hill of Mexican red ants.

Tarkey sighed like he was bored by the whole thing. "Ain't y'all finished yet? You gonna take all day?"

"Hey," called one of the men. "There's a woman in here."

"She dead?" Tarkey asked.

"She sure as hell looks to be."

The coach was lying on its side. Water rushed around it. Some of the debris had floated away, only to be recovered by the gang.

"Drag her out anyway," Tarkey said. "We can sell her dress to some of the Injuns around here."

"Ain't no Injuns—"

"Just drag her out."

They would have argued more, but they all heard the sounds of hooves coming toward them. The horses were running along the same bank where Tarkey stood. He gazed blankly toward the oncoming *remuda*.

"Bake is bringin' the horses," he said. "Guess he figured it was over."

One of the gang members was standing on the spokes of a coach wheel. He squinted toward the rushing animals. He started to say that the man behind the *remuda* didn't look like Bake. But then the rifle rang out and the man fell into the water clutching his chest. They all started to scramble for their weapons, but it was too late.

Slocum had arrived.

Slocum had tied the *remuda* together, charging them directly at the gang of bushwhackers. They formed a living wall of horseflesh between him and the guns that exploded, sending lead in his direction. He picked off the man on the wheel before the others could rally. But then they were shooting at him and the barricade of horses.

"Get him!" the leader cried.

Slocum took aim and fired at the man, hitting him in the leg. The leader went down clutching his thigh. The horses rushed over him, trampling his body with their hooves.

Slocum levered the Winchester, firing from the hip. The gang members were sitting ducks in the water. He cut down two of them with three shots. The others tried to hide behind the overturned vehicle.

"He's the devil!"

"Somebody get him."

"Holy Mercy, we're goners."

Slocum fired the last round from the rifle. He threw the weapon to the ground and drew the Peacemaker. He made a long circle on his mount, coming up behind the coach. The gang fired on him but they could not keep their balance in the stream.

The Peacemaker erupted in Slocum's hand. One man grabbed his throat and sank into the water. Slocum fired a slug between his shoulder blades to make sure he was dead.

Another bandit stood and fired in Slocum's direction. Slocum cut him down with a gut shot. The man collapsed into the water. Slocum sent a second chunk of lead into the back of the man's head.

There was only one man left. He raised his hands to the sky begging for mercy. He didn't want to die, he said.

"Don't want to die?" Slocum replied. "If you don't want to die, then why're you robbin' stagecoaches?"

"Please, mister. Don't—"

Slocum never had a single thought of mercy. "You didn't think nothin' 'bout killin' them on the stage. Did you?"

"I didn't want to hurt nobody. I don't even know why I did it now!"

"Nothin' like repentin' on the gallows," Slocum replied. "You ain't worth hangin'!"

The man tried to run, but he wasn't fast enough. He fell into the water, floating with the current. Slocum fired twice, hitting him both times. The blood flowed in the dark water, disappearing into the mud.

Slocum quickly reloaded the Peacemaker, making sure that none of them had survived. He dismounted and gazed toward the overturned stage. He hadn't cared much for the other passengers, but none of them had deserved such a sorry fate. He tried to feel better about avenging them, but the satisfaction didn't come easily. All the killing had left him with an aching in his gut.

Another shot rang out suddenly from behind him. Slocum felt a stinging in the upper part of his left arm. He turned to see the gang leader stumbling toward him with the rifle, trying to lever it for a second round. Slocum lifted the Peacemaker and shot the leader in the shoulder. The man dropped the Winchester but he did not fall.

"You bastard!" the man cried. "Who the hell are you?"

Slocum did not reply. The blood was trickling down his arm. The wound wasn't deep but it sure as hell hurt, even if the bullet had only grazed him.

"Go on," the leader said. "Shoot me."

Slocum lifted the Peacemaker, aiming at the man's chest.

"That's right," the leader went on. "Cut me down in cold blood."

"How's it any diff'rent than what you did to that stage?" Slocum challenged.

"It ain't."

Slocum's finger tightened on the trigger, but he could not bring himself to shoot the man. "All right," he said, holstering the Peacemaker. "You're wearin' a sidearm. Go on, reach for it."

The man stiffened in his tracks. He went for the gun on his hip, faster than he should have been able in his wounded state. Gun steel flashed in the morning light. But it wasn't fast enough.

Slocum's gun hand was quicker. He drew and fired, sending a slug into the middle of the leader's forehead. The man slumped forward, falling on his own weapon which discharged into his gut. His body shook as he died.

Slocum turned in a wide circle, waiting for another attack. It did not come. Everything was still except for the river and the horses that struggled to get loose of the tether holding them together. Slocum cut the ropes and let most of them free. Then he turned back toward the fallen coach, wondering what to do next.

7

Slocum stood like a statue for a long time, watching the rippled flow of the stream. The spring river split around the carcass of the coach. Several of the bodies had washed downstream, carried in the direction of Rock Springs, the town that Slocum now had to avoid. He didn't want any tangles with the local boys, even if the place was without a sheriff. Ordinary citizens could form lynching parties as quick as lawmen.

Gradually, he became aware of the wound on his arm. It had started to burn. He washed it in the river and then wrapped a crude bandage around his bicep. The scratch was the least of his worries. He had to figure out his next move. What was he going to do with a crippled stage and a river full of dead bodies?

As he backed away from the water, his leg bumped something on the bank. He gazed down at the strongbox. It was completely unharmed by the crash. The lock had been broken, but that had come from a rifle shot from the leader of the gang. Slocum figured he had to take a look, so he could see what all the killing had been about.

When he threw back the lid of the chest, the reflection of the sun almost blinded him. The box was full of gold double eagles. Who had been stupid enough to send so much gold on an overland stage? The money should have been accompanied by a regiment of troops, not one green lieutenant and a couple of hired guns. Maybe the sender had been counting on the fact that no one would suspect such a haul to be carted in such a haphazard manner.

Slocum looked around at the carnage again. Someone had known that the prize was on top of the stage. And there was something strange about the gang who had attempted the holdup. They didn't look like desperate bandits. They were more polished, like hired guns. Who hadn't wanted the stage to reach Rock Springs?

Slocum didn't care. It wasn't any of his business. He could just ride away, maybe head back east and then turn south.

He had a horse. He had guns. His eyes turned downward again. He also had a chest full of gold.

The gold weevil had burrowed into his brain. It was crawling around, making a nest, sowing its seeds. Just looking at the treasure had made Slocum a little dizzy. He knew how hard it was to hang on to large amounts of gold.

What if he took it with him? He could use four or five saddlebags and two of the *remuda* horses. It would be like carrying any other payload. He could pretend to be a miner until he got south. In New Mexico, he could tell people he was a horse trader made good. If he got new clothes, they'd believe him.

A shiver played through his body, ending at his shoulder blades. This much gold could attract a lot of scavengers from both sides of the law. Maybe it was best to just take a handful of eagles and be satisfied with that.

The same thought came back to him. What if the people in Rock Springs didn't know about the shipment of gold? If it had been a secret, then nobody would miss the strongbox for a long time. And the stage company didn't have Slocum's name. They didn't know he had been riding shotgun on the stage. All the other witnesses were dead.

His eyes were fixed on the metallic glimmer inside the chest. The gold was his for the taking. Who would know? If he rode hard for a couple of weeks, he could outrun anybody who might come after him.

"I'm gonna do it."

Load it up in saddle bags, take a packhorse, and try to make it to the Mexican border. If he could get to Nogales or Chihuahua, he could live like a king for the rest of his days. There had to be thousands in the trove. The hardest part would be figuring out how to spend it.

He caught another horse drinking by the river. It took eight saddle bags to carry the gold. The horse didn't like it when the burden went on his back. He kicked until Slocum persuaded him not to fight it.

Slocum then gathered every gun and all the ammunition he could find on the bank of the river. He tucked the leader's pistol in his belt, adding it to the Peacemaker that rode on his hip. He loaded the rifles and put two scabbards on the sling ring of his mount.

"Son of a bitch!"

He remembered that his own tack and belongings were somewhere in the wet cargo of the stage. But what did it matter? The saddle had been worn and the other things were so insignificant that he could not remember what had been his. He had the gold now. Everything else could be left behind.

He tied the reins of the packhorse to his saddle and then turned to survey the lay of the ground. East was the wrong direction, even if the road was the best that way. He'd leave tracks for anyone who might be looking for a surviving gang member.

Heading north didn't make much sense. He wanted to get the hell away from the spring misery. He had seen enough rain to last him a while. He couldn't remember what it was like to feel warm and dry.

Due west would take him into the town he wanted to avoid.

There didn't seem to be a trail directly to the south.

Southeast or southwest were the best bets. He settled on southwest, which would take him away from Rock Springs at an angle. He could take the mountain passes down into Utah.

He spurred the mount toward the southwest. The packhorse followed reluctantly. The ground was a little rocky, which meant no clear trail. He hoped he could outpace any danger by nightfall.

The sun was hanging low in front of Slocum. He hadn't really made good progress, but there didn't seem to be anyone after him. The horizon, or what he could see of it in the foothills, had remained empty. A couple of times, soaring birds had scared him a little, but then they would climb into the sky, something a rider couldn't do.

His packhorse was the problem. The big black gelding didn't like the dead weight of the gold. He kept trying to stop. Slocum thought about reversing the load and the saddle, but he decided he didn't want to ride the damned mean gelding.

All in all, he figured he was a good five miles from the wreck in the river, maybe a little less. As soon as he reached a place that had a mule for sale, he was going to trade the gelding outright for a better pack animal. Nothing, especially some hay burner, was going to keep him from making it to Mexico with the gold.

"Come on you mangy—"

The black snorted and reared. One of the saddlebags fell off onto the ground. Slocum had to dismount to pick it up. Several gold coins spilled onto the trail. He tried to grab them all and put them back in the leather pouch. Double eagles would leave a hell of a path for some lawman to follow.

Slocum's green eyes gazed again at his back trail. The air was calm, steady, almost warm. Nobody seemed to be after him. He climbed into the saddle again and fought his way through the rocks, hoping to make another couple of miles before it was too dark to ride.

When he finally stopped at nightfall, Slocum realized that he had not brought food or water with him. Gold did that to a man. It could make him forget about basic things. It filled his head with hateful thoughts.

"Maybe I oughta just ride on without it."

But that was not an option. So Slocum hunkered on a rock, leaning back against a slab of stone, closing his eyes. He slept dreamlessly until dawn, waking to an unexpectedly warm day. The sun was beating down on the rocks, sweating steam from the dampness.

His belly growled and his head spun, but when he remembered the gold, he mounted up and started into a narrow ravine. Utah couldn't be too much farther. And he had a warm day for traveling.

The black gelding even seemed to be cooperating. It followed him with little trouble. Maybe it was getting used to the load on its back. Slocum still planned to trade it for a mule.

The trail wound downward into a crevice. It was slow going, but Slocum managed to get through it. When he had cleared the

gorge and was moving on a wider trail, the black started to act
up again.

"Hyah!" Slocum cried, shaking the reins.

But the animal was set on being difficult. Dead set. It
began to rear and cry like a demon. Slocum looked back
to see dark, writhing shapes oozing out of the rocks like
worms. The damned black had stepped into a nest of rattlers.

The sun had awakened the snakes. Slocum's horse had
stirred them and now they were attacking the black with spring
hunger. Slocum drew his Colt, but it was useless. The rattlers
had struck the black's legs more than once.

Slocum used his pistol to finish off the horse. It fell into
the trail, scaring the snakes back into the rocks. Slocum dismounted, moving slowly toward the fallen animal with his
pistol cocked.

"Damned diamondbacks."

One of the creatures slithered out of the rocks, coming
directly at Slocum's feet. Slocum blew its head off with a
single burst from the Colt. The snake's severed body writhed
in a death dance.

"Anyone else want to try it?"

As he unloaded the saddle bags from the dead packhorse,
he kept watch for the rattlers. He managed to shoot one more
before they disappeared for good. Even a snake knew when it
was outmatched.

Slocum stared at the pile of saddlebags. Some of the coins
had spilled again. This time he didn't bother to pick them up.
He had to load the bags onto his mount. He'd have to walk
to Utah or until he found someone to sell him another pack
animal.

The trail seemed to be full of small rocks that made his feet
ache. He walked until midday, stopping for a siesta. As he
sat down, he noticed the blood on the horse's hoof. It would
be lame soon. Then what? He couldn't carry all the gold by
himself.

Slocum closed his eyes. His head swirled in a hazy, nightmare slumber. When he woke again, the sun was lower in
the sky. The heat had dissipated into the dampness of a cool
afternoon. Walking wouldn't be so bad if he traveled at night.
Even the snakes would be asleep then.

His mouth was dry. He'd have to find water soon. He continued on, walking the loaded mount. The way it was limping, it wouldn't last much longer. It was shaping up to be a bad damned idea to steal the gold.

The horse began to neigh and whinny. Slocum wondered if there was a pack of wolves hiding somewhere in the lowlands. That would make everything perfect for him. He drew his Colt again and forged on.

His animal had been excited about the smell of water. He rounded a craggy bend to find a dripping stream that ended in a pool. It was runoff from above, from the rains and the last of the melting snow.

Slocum drank beside the nuzzling horse. His belly cramped a little. He waited for the pain to subside and then drank again. The saddle carried an empty canteen that he filled immediately.

He had saved the two rattler carcasses. He skinned them, gutted the bodies, washed them, and then ate the meat raw. His body felt a lot better, but he was suddenly sleepy.

Sitting again, he closed his eyes and drifted off, still holding the reins of his horse. When he awoke in the cloudy afternoon, the animal was gone. Slocum stood quickly, heading down the trail, hoping he would find the horse alive.

His eyes grew wide when he saw the horse standing calmly in the middle of the path. It wasn't the mount that scared him. It was the stranger who stood holding the animal's reins. The man wore a narrow hat and a filthy duster.

"How do," the man said.

Slocum just nodded. Where the hell had he come from? Slocum couldn't see if the stranger wore a gun under his duster.

"This your horse?" the man asked.

"Yes."

He pointed at the horse's foreleg. "Going lame. Carrying a heavy load. Name's Rafferty. What're you doin' way out here?"

Slocum shrugged. "Might ask you the same thing."

The man moved around in front of the horse, squaring his shoulders to Slocum. He was a smallish, stocky man with a thick mustache. He could have been a trail robber or a U.S. marshal. Slocum had to find out which before he drew his gun.

The stranger nodded at the bandage on Slocum's arm. "Have some trouble?"

"Some."

The man smiled. "We all have trouble once in a while. Like the poor soul who lost this gold piece. Double eagle. Found a few back on the trail."

Slocum's hand drifted steadily toward his weapon.

Rafferty lifted a finger to point at him. "Don't try it, honcho. I'm not alone."

Slocum heard the echo of rifle levers. He looked up to see men beading down on him. There were scuffling boots on the trail behind him. Men with drawn pistols seemed to come out of the rocks.

"Hands to heaven," Rafferty said.

Slocum lifted his palms to the sky. "You're makin' a big mistake, mister. I ain't done nothin' wrong."

Rafferty came forward and took Slocum's handguns. "You're one lyin' son of a buck. Come on down, boys. Looks like we caught the man who robbed that stage. These saddlebags is full of gold."

Slocum counted a dozen in the posse, including Rafferty. They were all dressed in dusters and narrow-brimmed hats. A few of them wore suits and derbies. They had to be the good townspeople of Rock Springs. The posse had finally caught up to him.

Rafferty tipped back his hat. "He don't look like much. How'd you kill all them at the river?"

Slocum played dumb for the moment. He had to figure an angle. If he told them a huge lie, they might be more likely to believe him. He had to make it sound true.

"How'd you steal all that gold?" Rafferty went on. "You double-cross them boys you was ridin' with?"

"I wasn't ridin' with no one," Slocum replied. "And I wasn't plannin' to steal nothin'."

Rafferty gestured back toward the lame animal. "Them saddlebags say different. They're full of gold."

Slocum took a deep breath. "I was tryin' to bring them to Rock Springs," he said. "I got lost."

Rafferty got up in his face. "So you admit you was on that stage."

"I was."

"The inside man?" Rafferty asked.

Slocum nodded his head. "You could say that."

Rafferty put a finger in his face. "Aha! Then you admit you were in with those who attacked the stage."

"I don't admit no such," Slocum replied. "I was on that stage to protect the interests of the good people of Rock Springs."

"Come again?" Rafferty challenged. "You was protectin' their interests? How was you doin' that?"

"I'm Brick Hanson," Slocum replied. "I'm the new sheriff of Rock Springs. I was on my way into town when they attacked the stage."

Rafferty's mouth went slack. Slocum saw the doubt in his eyes. The tall man from Georgia had told a lie that could not be refuted. He hated to claim he was a lawman, but it seemed to be the only way out.

He nodded his head toward the horse. "When they attacked, I was thrown free. I ambushed their *remuda* man and gave it back to them."

That much was true.

Somebody hollered from the ring of men: "We did find that dead boy upstream. There was plenty of horse sign."

Another voice declared: "Aw, he ain't no sheriff. Look at him."

Rafferty had to shake his head. "Doggone it, who else coulda took all them men like that? Hanson was supposed to be tough."

Slocum thought he might be home free. At least they wouldn't lynch him right here if they bought his tall tale. He might have to give back the gold, but he would escape with his life.

"I was tryin' to bring that gold to town," Slocum went on. "But I got turned around. I musta missed Rock Springs. I thought I was headin' west, but I'm new out here. I don't know this territory too good."

"What about that man we found in the suit?" Rafferty asked.

Slocum's heart jumped. What if Hanson had been carrying some kind of papers on him? He'd be caught in the untruth and lynched from the nearest tree.

Slocum shrugged. "Some whiskey drummer, I reckon."

"That man didn't have no badge on him," someone called.

Rafferty nodded to a gray-haired man in a derby. "Mayor, what do you think?"

The man took a few steps toward Slocum. "I think there's one way to settle this," he said slowly. "Let the woman identify him."

Slocum's face went slack. Woman? It couldn't be. She couldn't have survived the crash of the coach.

"I forgot all about her," Rafferty said with a smile. "Miss Addie will surely be able to know her own husband. Come on, boy, let's go meet your wife."

And then we'll go meet the hangman, Slocum thought.

8

They put Slocum on a riderless mount and tied his hands to the saddle horn. As soon as they started back toward Rock Springs, the sky began to darken. A light rain fell on Slocum, chilling him again. The rain became harder, slopping up the trail and slowing the posse. Slocum hoped that it would take them forever to reach the mountain town. He knew he was sunk as soon as the woman saw his weathered face.

Rocking in the saddle, Slocum speculated as to what might happen to him once the truth became known. They would probably just hang him immediately. Of course, there could be a judge to hear the case, a circuit rider with the law book in one hand and the Good Book in the other. A trial would only delay the reckoning.

A judge might just send him to prison, but that would be worse than hanging. Wyoming's territorial jail was known to be one of the all time hellholes for killing prisoners. Nobody wanted to join that chain gang.

Slocum tried to think as the rain pelted him. He could stick with his story about trying to bring the gold back even after the woman identified him as an impostor. Hell, who would believe that? Any man would have larceny in his eyes with that golden reflection beaming off the sun.

Doomed. Riding to his hangman's noose. Slocum had always thought he would find his end from a stray bullet in a whorehouse gun battle. Now he was going to swing.

Slocum was surprised at how quickly they reached the wreck of the stagecoach. He hadn't traveled far at all. The gold had ruined his judgment. It was almost like a sickness had overtaken him.

The damned gold was only a few feet away, riding another horse, mocking Slocum with its siren's presence. He had been so close, or at least he had thought as much. How stupid he had been.

The posse stopped at the river, taking in the wreck one more time. Slocum looked for the woman until he realized that she had been transported back to town. Another slight delay in his demise. Why hadn't he listened to that little voice that had told him to ride on without the damned gold?

He turned his green eyes to the stage, which still lay on its side in the stream. How could Addie Hanson survive such a crash? Providence was playing a bad joke on the tall rebel from Georgia.

The man called Rafferty and the older man in the derby were also studying the wreck. Slocum figured they wore the big pants in Rock Springs. Rafferty had called the derby man "Mayor." They had sure put together the posse in a hurry. Slocum wondered what had tipped them off. Then he realized that the bodies from the wreck must have floated downstream into town. The current hadn't taken long to betray him.

Suddenly, the Mayor bent to the ground and picked up a thin scrap of paper. He studied it for a moment and then turned to walk back toward Slocum. The tall man squinted at the lined face. The Mayor looked up at him.

"You remember the letter I sent you . . . Hanson?" the man asked.

Slocum nodded. "I do."

"What did it say?"

Slocum sighed and shrugged. "I don't read too good, sir. My Addie read it to me. And I remember being grateful to you for giving me a chance to bring peace to your fine town."

The man tipped back his derby. "Hanson, if you are telling the truth, I want to apologize for all this. I'm Elmo Dunwood. That's Bob Rafferty. I'm the mayor of Rock Springs. Bob works for me."

"Glad to know you," Slocum replied.

He hated sucking up to town slickers, but he wanted to keep them on his side as much as possible. Maybe he could reason with them. No, the woman would ruin it as soon as she saw him.

Dunwood shook his head and sighed. "Bad business, this. I found part of that letter I sent you."

"Musta fallen out of my pocket," Slocum said.

Rafferty moved up next to his boss. "Mayor, we better get movin' again. We ain't got much daylight left at all."

Good, Slocum thought, at least they would arrive after dark. He wouldn't have to deal with the gathering crowds of gawkers who wanted to see the condemned man. The actual hanging would bring them out in droves, though.

Dunwood waved his hand over his head. "Move out, boys. We're gonna push through to town."

Slocum looked at the wreck one more time. How the hell had he gotten himself into this just by accepting a job on the stage? He might as well have stayed in Cheyenne. Either way, the result would have been the same.

The horses plodded toward Rock Springs in the rain. They kept moving even after the sun had disappeared from behind the clouds. Slocum figured they knew the trail well enough.

He glanced from side to side. Riders all around him. His hands tied to the saddle like a slaughter-bound pig. No chance for escape. Heading toward a certain appointment with his Maker.

Slocum looked to the dark sky, but the clouds did not open up. A dull roll of thunder played through the hollows of the foothills. Nobody was going to save him now. And he had almost forgotten how to pray.

Rock Springs seemed to come out of nowhere, rising up in the night, a dark monster with tiny lights for burning eyes. Slocum had underestimated the effect of his arrival on the townspeople. As they rode down the dirty main street, windows and doors opened so everyone could gaze upon the outlaw responsible for the bodies that had washed into town.

"Look, it's him."

"Aw, he ain't much."

"I wonder where they caught him."

Even in the rain, a small group gathered at the jail before the posse could tie up their horses. They shoved and gawked for a better look at Slocum. Yessiree, his hanging would be the event of the year. They'd be telling whoppers about the men Slocum had killed. His reputation would be legendary by the time the gallows trapdoor dropped open.

Rafferty turned back to glare at the mob. "Ain't no reason for y'all to be here. Get on home."

Mayor Dunwood also waved his fatherly hand. "Get gone, before I turn this posse on you!"

Slocum kept his eyes down as the crowd dispersed. Rafferty took his arm and turned him in the direction of the jailhouse. They put him in a ratty six-by-eight cell with a slop jar and a pail of water. Slocum hated the clinking sound of the cell door slamming shut.

He sat on the edge of a crude cot. Something ran out of the mattress, down his leg, and into the next cell. It was a two-hole jail. The other one was empty except for the fleeing vermin.

Rafferty and Dunwood stood there, gawking at him. They would soon know the truth. And Slocum had no bargaining power, not in a town that was so primed for a lynching. They wanted blood and the mayor was going to provide it for them.

"Think we ought to get the woman now?" Dunwood asked.

Rafferty shrugged. "It's late. She's probably sleeping."

Slocum leaned back against the wall. He wasn't anxious to see Addie Hanson. The angel of death, she was, a harpy from the bowels of Satan's territory. She might as well be the one pulling the rope for the trapdoor.

"You want something to eat, Hanson?" Dunwood asked.

Slocum sighed with fatigue. "Sure."

His last meal.

"Rafferty," Dunwood said, "get one of those men of yours to go over to the hotel. Round up some food for all of us."

Rafferty shook his head. "They won't like openin' the kitchen this late."

Dunwood glared at him. "Have you forgotten that I own the hotel?"

"No, but I—"

"Just do it!" Dunwood snapped.

Rafferty stomped out, grousing under his breath. Slocum realized Dunwood was definitely the one in charge. He might also be the one to reason with in order to save his neck.

Slocum considered telling the truth right then, begging for mercy. But he figured it wouldn't do much good. Better just to play it out. Maybe the widow Hanson would die in the night.

Dunwood gazed through the bars of the cell. "If you are Hanson, then we have a lot of talking to do."

Slocum just nodded. What could he say? He wasn't Hanson and pretty soon everyone in Rock Springs would know it.

There was scuffling in the outer office of the jail. One of the posse men came in, calling to Mayor Dunwood. He wanted to know what to do with the gold. It was still in the saddlebags outside.

"Shut your fool mouth," Dunwood snapped at the man. "Do you want the whole damned town to hear you?"

Slocum's ears pricked at the tone of Dunwood's voice.

"Put it back in the strongbox in my office and stay there with it until I tell you different," Dunwood said in a lower voice. "And don't say a word about it to anyone, do you hear? That's what I'm paying you for. Your silence."

The man disappeared out the front door. Slocum had to laugh. The mayor was stealing the money. Unless it was his to begin with. Whatever the situation, Dunwood didn't want anyone to know about the gold.

They left Slocum alone until the food arrived from the hotel. Rafferty slid a tray under the cell door. Slocum ate a rich, dark stew and some corn bread. He wondered how many good meals he would get before the hanging.

In the office, Dunwood and Rafferty talked in low, conspiratorial voices. They were sure as hell up to something. They had a lot of manpower in the riders that had taken Slocum. What the hell did they need with a sheriff?

Suddenly Rafferty's voice rose up. "Hey, you can't come in here!"

Mayor Dunwood was right behind him. "Leave her be."

A woman's sweet tone filled the jailhouse. "My Brick. Where is he? They say he was saved."

Slocum suddenly felt like vomiting. The widow Hanson had arrived early. Someone had awakened her with the news of her husband's safety. Now she was going to finish the tall man from Dixie.

"I heard my Brick was here," she went on. "I want to see him, to kiss his sweet face."

"All right," Rafferty said. "Come on, we might as well get it over with. He's in there."

A light glowed in the mayor's hand as they came through the doorway. Addie Hanson was wearing some sort of robe. She pressed her face to the cell bars and looked in at Slocum.

"Turn your face into the light so she can see you," Dunwood said.

Slocum had to obey. A dull luster appeared in his green eyes. He looked the widow squarely in the face.

"No!" Addie Hanson cried.

Rafferty smiled. "See, I told you it wasn't him. He's been a lyin' son of a bitch all along."

Slocum sank back on the cot. He wondered if they would start building the gallows right away. If he was lucky, he might get enough time to plot an escape attempt. He had busted out of jails before.

Mayor Dunwood put his hand on Addie's shoulder. "Come on, Mrs. Hanson. I'll see you back to the hotel."

"No!" Addie cried again. "You aren't taking me away from my Brick."

Dunwood's eyes narrowed. "What?"

Addie winked at Slocum. "Oh, Brick. I can't believe you survived. I thought for sure you'd be dead."

Rafferty put his hands on his hips. "You mean to tell me that this roughcut trail bum is your husband?"

Addie wheeled around to indict him with a hateful look. "You be careful how you talk about my Brick."

Slocum could not believe what he was hearing. Maybe the damned woman had gone *loco*. But when she turned back to him, she winked again, letting him in on the deception. What the hell was she doing? And why was she doing it?

"Oh, Brick, honey, I dreamed you was dead, that you were in heaven. What happened, Brick? Why did you go away?"

Slocum saw the opening. "I was tryin' to bring that gold back to town, Addie. I thought you were a goner. So I wanted to do my duty to the fine folks of Rock Springs."

Crocodile tears ran down her cheeks. "I knew you were a good man, honey. You'll be the best sheriff this town ever had."

Slocum didn't like the sound of that, but it was better than hanging. He wasn't sure how the hand would fall, but he had to keep playing the cards. Addie was his queen of hearts. His winning card out of Rock Springs.

"Come here and kiss me," Addie said.

Slocum lowered his head. "I can't, Addie. I'm too ashamed of being in this jail. They think I wanted to steal that gold."

Addie turned to the powers-that-be, glaring with indignation. "How dare you accuse my husband of such things?"

Rafferty and Dunwood shifted nervously on their feet. They hadn't been prepared for Addie's reaction. They didn't know how to deal with an irate woman whose "husband" had been locked away.

She pointed at the jail door. "Free him this minute!"

Rafferty grimaced. "Are you sure about this?"

"I know my own husband!"

Dunwood nodded toward the lock. "Let him go."

"I don't know, Mayor," Rafferty said.

"Go on."

Rafferty turned the key in the door. "You're free to go, Hanson."

Slocum got up and started toward the opening. Addie ran in and threw her arms around him. She began to kiss his face and lips. The other two men turned away in embarrassment.

Slocum's lips brushed her ear. "What the hell is goin' on?"

"Play along," Addie whispered. "I'll tell you all about it later."

"I thought for sure he was lyin'," Rafferty muttered.

Dunwood shot him a dirty look. "Quiet. Mr. Hanson, I hope you will accept my apologies for the confusion. As a man of the law, I'm sure you understand."

Slocum grimaced at the mayor. "I ain't one to hold a grudge, Dunwood."

"Glad to hear it, sir. And here's your gun. Now, if you'll allow me, I'll escort you and your bride back to the hotel."

Addie smiled at Dunwood. "Thank you so much, sir. I'll never forget what you've done for us."

The expression on Rafferty's face betrayed his skepticism. "I'll go with them, Mayor."

"You don't have to," Slocum offered. "Addie and me can find our way."

Slocum figured to skedaddle as soon as nobody was looking, even if he had to walk out of town. The woman had gotten him out of trouble for the moment, but he could still fall back into the fire. What if there were wanted posters on him in Rock Springs? Of course, if he was the sheriff, he could throw away any poster that vaguely resembled his description.

A lawman! It would burn a hole in his gut. No, he had to wait for the right moment and bolt. He wouldn't rest until he was safely out of Wyoming.

Rafferty made a mocking bow and a sweeping gesture. "After you, Hanson. We want to make sure you're comfortable at the hotel."

There was no getting shed of them, Slocum thought. They followed him and Addies across the dirty street to the hotel. It was a clean, bright, little place, better than Slocum had known in a while. Rafferty and Dunwood even followed them upstairs to the room where Addie had been sleeping.

Addie took Slocum's arm. "Thank you so much, gentlemen. I'll give him back to you in the morning."

"See that you do," Rafferty replied curtly.

Dunwood nodded back toward the stairs. "See to your duties, Rafferty," the mayor snapped. "The sheriff has to rest now."

Slocum nodded. "Much obliged."

Rafferty turned and walked away, but he did not go down the stairs. Instead, he hesitated to wait for Dunwood. It was obvious that he didn't trust Slocum or the woman.

Dunwood's face appeared mean and sinister in the shadows. "Sheriff Hanson, we have much to discuss in the morning. I'll call for you."

"Sure," Slocum replied, even though he had no intention of being there.

Addie opened the door. "Come on, Brick." She pulled Slocum inside the room.

As soon as the door was shut, Slocum put his ear to the wood.

"Honey," Addie said. "I—"

"Hush!"

Slocum listened to the faint voices in the hall.

"I'm tellin' you," Rafferty insisted, "that ain't Hanson."

"We need him," Dunwood replied. "Now come on, we have work to do."

Their boots clomped on the stairs as they went down.

Slocum took a deep breath and turned to the woman. He was going to thank her. Then he saw that the smile had disappeared from her face. She clutched the front of her robe with trembling hands.

"Okay," Slocum said softly, "s'pose you tell me what's goin' on here."

9

The widow Hanson began to cry. She was good at calling up a sorrowful nature. Tears stained her pretty round face, her full mouth trembled. She touched her breast with a quivering hand. The sobbing appeared to come from deep within her, but Slocum did not believe her for a second. She had changed directions too quickly. Addie could put on a hell of an act, he thought. Look at the way she had convinced Dunwood and Rafferty that Slocum was really her long lost lawman husband. That kind of talent could prove deadly.

"It was horrible," she whimpered. "Brick dying like that. I was terrified when they were shooting at us."

Slocum folded his arms, watching her with narrow eyes. She wasn't the kind to evoke sympathy in him. Perching on the edge of the bed, she parted her legs slightly as she cried. The air was dangerously heavy with the odor of her perfume. Slocum had to be careful with this one.

Her large, dark eyes focused on the tall man from Georgia. "Would you come sit beside me?"

He shook his head. He didn't say a word. He wanted to see where the widow was taking this whole thing.

Addie jumped to her feet, coming toward him. "Oh, it was the most horrible nightmare."

She pushed herself against him, wrapping her arms around his torso. Her face rested on his chest. The perfume almost choked him.

"Hold me," she murmured. "Just hold me."

Slocum let her rest there for a moment before he pushed her firmly away from him. "Rein back, Addie. I ain't buyin' today."

She played the confused little girl. "What? I don't—"

He took off his hat, tossing it over a hook on the back of the door. "Don't say another word till you're ready to tell me what you're up to, Addie."

She wheeled away from him, huffing and snorting, showing him her broad backside. "How dare you talk to me like that!"

Slocum slumped down into a padded chair. "You change horses too much, honey. You got a swindle going. Who's the sucker? Me?"

Addie shuddered and sighed. Her body went limp. She suddenly seemed to lose all her strength. She steadied herself against a dresser.

"I'm so tired," she said softly. "So very tired."

Slocum guffawed and propped up his feet on the edge of the bed. "Why'd you vouch for me, Addie? Why'd you say I was your husband?"

Addie did not reply. She pulled open a dresser drawer. Slocum thought she might be going for a weapon. He drew his Colt and thumbed the hammer.

The widow turned to gape at the bore of the Peacemaker. "Cowboy!"

Slocum saw that she had a bottle of whiskey in her hand. He lowered the weapon, resting it on the arm of the chair. He figured he was never going to trust her.

Addie uncorked the bottle. She drew a long swig, guzzling like a dance-hall rummy. She wiped her mouth with the back of her hand and then thrust the bottle toward Slocum.

A healthy swallow burned the lining of his gullet. It was smooth liquor, not the local corn and rotgut potions. A second shot made him feel a whole lot warmer. It had been a cold trail to Rock Springs.

"Where'd you get this Kentucky creekwater?" Slocum asked.

Addie shrugged and then helped herself to another drink. "These town hay shakers have been waitin' on me hand and foot. They give me anything I want. Hell, half of them want to marry me right now."

Slocum chortled. Now they were getting closer to the truth. All the sorrow and regret had disappeared from her voice.

She scowled at him. "Don't grin at me. You knew right from the start, didn't you? You had me spotted on the stage. You smug bastard."

"I didn't say anything, honey."

"Don't call me honey," she replied contemptuously. "I'm a Kansas City chippy. A stockyard baby from dusk till dawn. Been makin' my livin' on my back since I was wet behind the ears."

"You don't have to give testimony to me," Slocum offered. "I ain't judgin' you for it."

"Brick knew what I was," she went on sadly. "He arrested me a couple of times when he was a constable. He liked me for some reason. But we couldn't stay in K.C., not with my reputation, so he took the job here. Now he's dead. And I don't even miss him."

"You still ain't told me why you claimed I was your husband," Slocum challenged.

She took a deep breath and another drink. "I didn't love Brick. He was good to me, though. Never wanted too much in bed. Just did his business and got off. He even acted like a gentleman most of the time."

"Don't change the subject," Slocum told her. "Tell me why you lied for me? Why'd you come runnin' to that jailhouse?"

A sly smile barely cracked her full lips. "You were in trouble, weren't you? Big trouble."

Slocum frowned. She had him cornered there. Like it or not, she had saved his life with her little ruse. He owed her. But what the hell was she going to ask in repayment? Probably too much.

"I helped you," she went on. "They would've kept you in that jail if I hadn't come along. Now you may have to help me."

"I ain't got nothin' to give you, woman."

She darted across the room, kneeling next to the chair. "Don't you see, cowboy, I'm not worth anything around this town without a husband. I ain't goin' back to whoring. Brick was supposed to get a good wage here. They promised us a house after six months."

Slocum shook his head. "No."

"You don't even know what I've got to say," she replied. "Just listen to me for a second."

Slocum wasn't about to throw in with some stupid deception. "I can see it comin', Addie. I ain't gonna be your husband. It'd be foolish to try."

"It wouldn't have to be for long," she pleaded. "Just until I get the house. Then you can disappear and I can get a widow's pension. I know we could do it, cowboy. These local boys aren't very bright."

"Don't sell 'em short," Slocum replied. "Rafferty still doesn't believe that I'm Brick Hanson."

"You could convince him different, cowboy."

Slocum glared at her. "No!"

She stood up, peering angrily into his face. "The way I see it, you ain't got much choice. You owe me. You'll give me what I want."

"I couldn't pretend to be a lawman," he replied. "I hate sheriffs and marshals and bounty hunters. I can't be a lawman. It goes against my beliefs."

"Just a few weeks," she whined. "Let me draw an advance on his pay if nothin' else. Then I can get the hell out of here."

"An advance, huh?"

Slocum understood her reasoning. Maybe he could swindle a few double eagles out of the town himself. Then he could get the devil out of Rock Springs. The quicker he could leave, the better. The way Dunwood and Rafferty were skulking around, there had to be some trouble brewing. And they seemed to want to put the new sheriff in the middle of it.

"I hate this place," Addie moaned.

"Then why'd you leave Kansas City?"

She knelt next to him again. "Don't you see, I had to start over. If Brick stayed alive, we had his pay. If he got killed, then I collect the widow's pension. Dunwood promised the pension if Brick died."

"He's dead."

"Oh, they'll never pay me now. He died before he started the job. Besides, they think you're Brick."

"There ain't no reason to be happy about that."

Addie ran her hands over his shoulders, rubbing the sore spots. "I'd hate for them to learn who you really are. I mean,

some thought you were stealing that money. Who knows what
they'd do if they learned the truth? I'd hate to see something
bad happen to you."

Slocum's eyes narrowed. "You threatenin' me?"

She smiled. "No. I just think we have to stick together.
Anything that happens to one of us happens to the other. You
understand?"

A burning pain seared the inside of his chest. Addie was
right. They had become partners of a sort. Slocum hated being
partners with anyone, especially a woman he couldn't trust.

He had to ride out before things got too thick. Addie was bad
luck. Look at the ill fortune she had brought her husband.

Addie brushed his cheek with her full lips. "We're man and
wife now, cowboy. Want to have me in the marriage bed? I
mean, all this excitement has got me worked up. I'm wet."

Slocum smiled for a moment but then pushed her away.
She tumbled onto her well-rounded backside. The robe fell
open to reveal the pink nightgown beneath the heavy fabric. She was a fine woman, but somehow he didn't feel the
urge.

"I told you, Addie, I ain't buyin'."

She jumped to her feet, closing the robe. "What's wrong
with you? When we were on the stage, you couldn't keep
your eyes off my tits. Don't you want me? Don't you think
I'm pretty?"

"I got respect for widows," he offered with a sly smirk.

She pointed a finger at him. "I'll show you. I'll tell Dunwood
and Rafferty who you really are."

She started for the door.

Slocum shrugged. "A double hanging. They'll come from
the Dakotas when they hear a woman is going to swing."

She stopped in her tracks. "I need another drink." She gulped
from the whiskey bottle.

Slocum declined another shot. His head was already spin-
ning too much. He had work to do and he didn't need his
senses dulled.

"What's wrong with you?" the woman asked bitterly. "You
turn into a lily-livered mama's boy?"

Slocum stood up, slipping the Peacemaker into the holster.
"I'm gonna scout this place. You stay here and nurse that
bottle."

Again she latched on to him, holding him desperately. She wanted to take advantage of him with her body. She wanted to come along for the ride. Slocum thought it was probably best to leave her behind. She would only slow him up in the long run. Still, he had to repay her for saving his ass.

She gazed into his eyes. "You're leaving, aren't you?"

Slocum looked away.

Her face buried into his chest. "Take me with you. Don't leave me in this hellhole. I don't want to go back to working."

He broke off the embrace. "You just stay put till I get back."

"I'll be right here, darling."

Slocum wondered what it might be like with her. Of course, he could just as well bed down with a rattler. Even in the wake of her perfume, he still felt that she would strike him sooner or later. Who could blame her? They both had to look out for their own selves.

Taking his hat from the back of the door, Slocum turned the doorknob and then eased into the hall. He hesitated for a moment, putting his hat on his head. He wanted to be ready to move if he saw an opening. He didn't like the idea of horse-stealing, a hanging crime, but it might take that to get the hell out of Rock Springs.

Closing the door, he stole to the edge of the stairwell, looking down into the lobby. A lone light burned, casting orange streaks on the bottom stair. Slocum saw the glint on a pair of boots. Somebody was loitering in the night. Dunwood and Rafferty had left a sentry.

Slocum called to the man, scaring him. The man looked up the stairs. Slocum could not see his eyes under the brim of the hat.

"Is Mr. Dunwood still here?" Slocum asked.

He wanted it to appear like he had a real reason for coming out of the room.

The man shook his head. "Nope, he's gone."

Slocum tipped his own hat. "Much obliged. Sorry I scared you."

"It's all right," the man replied.

Slocum backed away into the hall. One sentry at the bottom of the stairs. He returned to the room where the woman smiled at him. He ignored her, going to the window and lifting it open.

Sticking his head through the casement, he peered out into the darkness. He did not see the man but he could hear him shuffling. He also smelled the tobacco smoke in the air. A guard in the back alley.

He went into the hall looking for another way out. There was a door against the south wall. He opened it to find a second set of steps leading upward. Slocum mounted the dark stairwell with slow steps.

Another door awaited him at the top. He threw it open and stepped out onto the roof of the building. He could see all of Rock Springs. The town was dim and misty.

For a long time, he walked the perimeter of the roof, gazing down at the streets of the town. There were at least two or three more men, probably the members of the posse, stirring in the shadows. They wanted to keep an eye on the new sheriff. Or was it something else?

Slocum saw a light swell to brightness in a building across the street. He could barely make out the sign on the facade: Dunwood Mining. Beneath it was another sign: Dunwood Team Hauling.

Dunwood was the town money man. He seemed clearly in control. Rafferty and the posse were on his payroll. Why did he need a sheriff?

Two figures appeared in the window of the mining offices. Slocum saw Dunwood and Rafferty talking. They seemed to be in a heated discussion. Slocum could not hear what they were saying, but he recognized a fight when he saw one. Rafferty finally stomped out and closed the door.

Easing back from the edge of the roof, Slocum watched as Rafferty came out onto the street. Two men ran to greet him. They were giving him a report, probably telling him that Slocum had come out of the room looking for Dunwood.

Rafferty listened and then stormed off down the street. Slocum thought he had seen the last of him. But Rafferty decided to turn around and come back toward the hotel.

"Damn!"

Slocum didn't feel like dealing with Rafferty. He started across the roof, climbing down the stairs, closing all the doors behind him. When he burst into the room, he startled the woman. She was already under the covers.

"What is it?" she asked.

Slocum lifted a finger. "Shh."

He listened for Rafferty but there were no immediate foot-steps on the stairs.

Voices rose out of the back alley, filtering through the open window. Slocum stood next to the casement. He could hear Rafferty talking with one of the sentries.

"Anything?"

"No, sir."

Rafferty scoffed. "They ain't doin' it?"

"Ain't heard a sound, Mr. Rafferty. He opened the window a while ago, but I ain't heard nothin' more."

Rafferty laughed. "I told you they weren't man and wife. I'm going up there. I'm going to fix that stranger once and for all."

Slocum shook his head. Did Rafferty think he couldn't be heard? Maybe he didn't care.

"What's going on?" Addie asked behind her covers.

"We're gonna have some company," Slocum replied.

"What do you mean?"

"Somebody else is interested in our marriage bed. And we got to make him think we're in love."

Addie's face betrayed her confusion. "What?"

Slocum drew back the bedclothes. "Scoot over."

"I don't understand."

Rafferty's boots had begun to tap on the wooden stairs.

"Make like you're havin' a good time," Slocum said. "Moan and rattle some bedsprings."

"Why?"

"Just do it!"

They began to shake their bodies. Addie made noises that she had learned in her years of working. They rolled together in the middle of the bed, bumping their bellies.

Outside in the hall, Rafferty paused with his fist ready to knock. But when he heard the sounds of passion, he lowered his arm. Something still didn't feel right, but he was not about to interrupt a man and his wife when they were doing *that*.

He wheeled away, marching down the hall to the stairs.

Slocum stopped next to the woman. "Shh. Listen, he's gone. He—"

"Shut up, cowboy. Shut up and screw me."

10

The widow Hanson rolled over on top of Slocum, kissing his face with her full, moist lips. Her tongue worked its way over his mouth, probing and licking. She squirmed on him, a pleasant, living weight with huge breasts. And there was no way to resist her. The action had him all worked up. And she knew it.

Her hand grabbed his crotch. "Let's see you deny me now."

She stroked the hardness. Slocum let her do it. She didn't take long to unbutton his pants, freeing him to the bare warmth of her touch.

"This don't mean nothin'," he said hoarsely.

Addie dipped her head, taking him into her mouth. His body went rigid. She was a real pro. No nonsense, just get down to business. Hanson had lost himself a hell of a wife.

She removed herself, smiling at him. "I want you on top. Fast, hard, and deep. Don't hold back."

Reclining on the bed, she hiked up the robe and the night-gown, giving him a flash of her large, white thighs. Ladybell hadn't been any more appealing. Slocum felt himself caving in a little.

"I want it, cowboy."

She grabbed his shoulders, pulling him on top of her. Her hand guided him into position. As Slocum thrust downward, the woman pushed up. His member sank deep into her open flower.

"That's it," she coached. "Yeah, keep it in me even after you shoot."

Slocum moved up and down, driving home the railroad spike. Addie bounced with him, wrapping her legs around his waist. He tried to hold back but it was too late. The dam was ready to break.

Addie cried out when he released. She drew her legs tightly together, holding him inside. His cock pulsed in the moist walls of her pink crevice.

"Don't pull out," she whispered. "Stay on me. Can you do it again?"

Slocum wasn't sure. He pulled out, lying on his back. Addie went to work again. She coaxed him to life with tricks he had never seen before.

As soon as he was hard, she shifted her body, climbing onto all fours. "Like the stallion and the mare," she said. "Hard again."

He got up behind her, gazing down at her plump ass. If nothing else, at least he was having luck with whores. First Ladybell and then the pride of Kansas City. He wondered if she had given it to the sheriff like this.

She reached back, grabbing his cock, resting the head at the entrance to her femininity. Before he could thrust in, she rocked back, taking his entire length. Her ass jiggled as she worked his Johnson like a new pump handle.

"Let me have it," she moaned. "Give it to me."

A proud working girl, Slocum thought. Addie really seemed to want it. Sometimes even whores had to have the genuine article.

Grabbing her hips a little tighter, he brought it home again. She arched her back and howled like coyote when he shot. Those noises would keep the sentries convinced that they were married. It would probably make them horny too.

Slocum collapsed on the mattress. Addie fell next to him. She grabbed his head and pulled it toward her breasts.

"Suck my titties. Just for a moment."

Slocum nursed like a baby. The suckling seemed to send waves of pleasure through her lovely body. She had taken good care of herself. A lot of whores turned to liquor when they got older and it usually showed. Addie appeared to be capable of holding her rotgut.

"We can help each other," she said softly.

Slocum drew back. Here it came again. The swindle. She wasn't going to let up on him for a minute.

"They were going to pay Brick three hundred a month," she offered.

Slocum felt his interest rising. "Three hundred?"

"That's what they said."

He thought about the money. If he could pull off a month in Rock Springs, he'd have a good traveling grubstake. No! He couldn't be a sheriff, not even a pretend one. It just went strictly against his nature.

"Three hundred," she repeated.

That kind of money drew trouble. They wouldn't be paying ten times what a local lawman was worth if the town was peaceful.

If he could fool them for a day or two, he might get an advance and a horse out of them. That would be better than nothing. Take off, ride hard, let the widowed lady fend for herself. Hell, if Addie was smart, she could be running the place in a couple of months. She already had the town eating from her hand.

"You could fake your own death," she went on. "That way I'd have my pension and you could leave."

Slocum slapped her on the thigh. "Don't be jokin' about death."

"I'm not joking. I—"

"Hush up," he said. "Get some sleep."

Addie didn't protest any. She dropped off quickly, snoring through her open mouth. Slocum fought the urge to like her. They had a lot in common. For one thing, they were both trapped in Rock Springs.

Climbing off the bed, he went to the window where he heard movement in the alley. Cigarette smoke filled the cool air. Dunwood's men were not going away.

He still couldn't figure out why they needed a sheriff with so much hired iron in town. Slocum wondered what had happened to the last sheriff. Lawmen usually didn't live too long in the mining towns. There was too much stray lead, too many crazed yahoos.

He buttoned his pants and eased out into the hall, tiptoeing to the edge of the stairwell. The guard leaned against the wall, his eyes closed. If Dunwood was paying a sheriff three hundred, what could he be paying the men in the dusters?

Sheriff. Slocum had always hated the very word. Lawmen were always rousing drifters, running them out of town. They just couldn't seem to stand seeing a man be free.

But where the hell else could he go? Leaving Rock Springs with no horse and no money would be fatal. No man should push his luck that far.

How much luck would he have if he played out the game with Dunwood and Rafferty? They had him surrounded. Slocum figured that Dunwood, like Rafferty, probably had his doubts about Slocum and the woman.

So why did Dunwood want Slocum to become sheriff? Did they need a scapegoat? And what about the money that now rested in a new strongbox in Dunwood's office? The chest full of gold had once belonged to Slocum. Did he have a chance to get it back? He probably had as much right to the double eagles as Dunwood.

Back in the room, he sat down in the chair, trying to figure a plan, a path to take. Like it or not, he had to play along with Dunwood for a while. They couldn't keep an eye on him forever. If he lured them into trusting him, they might give him a freer hand. Then he could run like a scared rabbit.

"Sheriff." He said the word with resignation.

Addie stirred on the bed. "Huh?"

"Nothin'. Go back to sleep."

The more he thought about it, the clearer it became that Dunwood was afraid of someone or something. Why else would he have so much firepower around him? He had sure snatched up that gold in a hurry.

Slocum still saw the yellow glint in his eyes. The sun had reflected so lovingly off the shiny coins. His heart beat faster just thinking about it.

The woman moaned in her sleep, writhing on the bedclothes. Slocum began to wonder how helpful she might be in stealing the gold back. Was he really going to try it? Maybe, if the time was right and the situation not too dangerous. Otherwise, getting out of town was the most important thing, the final step of his scheme.

His eyes stayed on Addie. She was tossing around like she was having a bad dream. Her legs parted for a moment. He caught a flash of her dark patch.

"Damn."

Just seeing her had made him hard again. Why did she have to smell so good? If he kept mounting her proper-like, she'd never leave him alone. Still, it had been a few days since Cheyenne, so he was ready and there it was.

After stripping down to his birthday suit, he climbed back into bed with her, rolling between her legs. She woke up when he penetrated her. She was numb at first but then, quickly, she caught on and humped him back.

They were sweating by the time he shot again. She held him inside her until he was soft. Slocum rolled off, trying to catch his breath.

"Better watch out," she said. "I might start to love you."

"You'd be a fool if you did."

She laughed and closed her eyes. "Go to sleep."

Slocum was also spent. No matter what he faced in the morning, it would look a lot better after some rest. He drew a pillow behind his head and fell instantly into a deathlike slumber.

"Sheriff, it's time to wake up."

The knocking stirred Slocum from his coma. He sat up, frowning. He thought he had heard someone calling for the sheriff.

The hand persisted, knuckling on the door. "Sheriff Hanson, it's time to get up. Mr. Dunwood wants to see you."

Hanson! Slocum remembered that he was now thought to be a deceased lawman from Kansas City. Addie had lied for him, saving him from the noose. She lay snoring next to him, oblivious to the noise in the hallway.

"Damn."

"Are you in there, Sheriff Hanson?"

"You know I am. Gimme a while."

The man paused. "Er, we don't have a while. Mr. Dunwood wants to see you. And we got some other things to do before you meet with him."

Slocum put his feet on the floor. "I'll come when I'm ready. Wait for me downstairs."

The man let out a sigh of impatience. "All right. But hurry. We have to be at Mr. Dunwood's office in an hour."

An hour? Slocum wondered what they were going to do in the meantime. Maybe it was some kind of trap. As soon as he was dressed, he strapped on his six-shooter. He wasn't going anywhere without the Peacemaker.

Addie stirred in bed, wakened by his clomping. "Where are you going?"

"To meet with Dunwood," he replied.

She sat up. "Don't forget to ask for a week's advance on your pay. No, ask for two and take one. And if they press you for details, tell them that you don't want to talk about Kansas City."

He hesitated, gazing into her hopeful face. She might be able to help him. She was smart and had a flair for trickery. He considered telling her right then about the gold, but he figured she probably knew.

"What?" she asked, squirming under his scrutiny.

He shrugged. "I ain't promisin' nothin', but let's see how this goes. We might both get a chance to leave this place."

She grinned. "I knew I could count on you."

Slocum headed downstairs. The young man in the duster was waiting for him. He introduced himself to Slocum as Hud Jones. His face was still smooth, almost beardless—a young buck looking for excitement.

"Can I call you Sheriff?" Jones asked.

"No. Don't call me nothin'. Just tell me where we're goin'."

Jones gestured toward the street. "Nothin', really, just that Mr. Dunwood thought you might like to get cleaned up before you meet with him. You got credit at the bathhouse and the general store. He thought you might want some new clothes and a pair of boots."

"Can't pass that up," Slocum replied.

Might as well milk it while he had the good hand. Things would not go so easy when the cards were finally on the table. How long would it take for Dunwood to call his hand?

They started outside. Rock Springs was a narrow, dirty, little town. The sun was shining, but the streets had not yet dried. Everything seemed to be stuck in the mire.

"You're from Kansas City, huh?" Jones asked.

Slocum kept his eyes on the street, ignoring the kid. He saw a sign that read "Dunwood's Saloon" and another that rendered ownership of the local feed and grain to Dunwood, though the feed store was closed. Not much room for farmers in a mining town.

He bathed and shaved at a bathhouse owned by Dunwood. The barber who cut his hair talked of nothing but Mr. Dunwood. He bought his clothes at the Dunwood General Store, where the clerk stopped everything to serve him at Mr. Dunwood's request.

"The town sugar-tit," Slocum muttered as he walked toward the offices of Dunwood mining.

Jones squinted at him. "Huh?"

"Don't you never shut up, kid?"

Jones reached into his pocket. "Here, you might as well put this on. You're gonna need it."

Slocum stopped, gazing into the kid's outstretched palm. He caught the dull luster of the tin star. The word "Sheriff" had been etched across the badge. Slocum's stomach turned at the sight of it.

"Don't you want it?" Jones asked.

Slocum shook his head, turning away. "Not just yet. I got to listen to Dunwood first."

As he turned away from the kid, Slocum suddenly saw his reflection in a glass window in Dunwood's office door. He did not recognize the clean, well-groomed stranger who looked back at him. Only the beat-up hat belonged to John Slocum. The rest of it belonged to someone else.

After Slocum had left the hotel room, Addie Hanson sat for a while trying to figure out her own plight. She had her doubts about the tall, lean cowboy. Men like him could bolt in a hurry. They could be down the trail before their dicks were dry.

So far, the other men in town seemed like slim pickings. Rafferty wasn't bad, but he was just some hired gun. The real money lay in the coffers of Mayor Dunwood. But he didn't seem to be interested in her.

Addie lay back on the bed, looking at the ceiling. The cowboy had ridden her fine. She hadn't wanted it like that for a long time.

But she knew she couldn't judge a man just by the way he topped her. Men didn't have feelings about *that*. Addie had not experienced *those* feelings for a good while. Somehow, the cowboy brought it out in her. She reminded herself to ask his name. She had forgotten it in the shuffle.

"Rock Springs," she said aloud.

It had been a mistake to come west, but now she had to make the best of it. Dunwood's letter to her late husband had promised an account at the local general store. Maybe she could buy herself a dress and some other niceties. Most of her possessions had been lost in the wreck. She'd have to start all over.

The one dress that had been rescued from the coach was a frilly blue gown that hardly seemed right for a one-horse mining town. She got up, making the best of the primitive conditions.

Maybe she could start a cathouse in Rock Springs. Hell, if there was a whorehouse within a hundred miles, Dunwood probably owned it. Maybe that would be her best approach to the old boy, a business deal. He looked like the type that could always use a profit.

"Addie, you're gonna do yourself right today."

She went downstairs where the hotel cook fed her a big breakfast. Every man in the place managed to slide by her table. But not one of them spoke. She was the sheriff's wife. The best they could do was to court the widow after the sheriff got killed.

Addie hated to think of the cowboy in a pine box, but she knew it would happen. There had to be a sacrifice. Why not the lanky rebel? He was a hostile trail bum, even if he was hung like a donkey.

As she left the breakfast table, she caught sight of Slocum and the young man in the duster. They were standing at the office door of the Dunwood Mining Company. Why was the cowboy hesitating?

She saw the boy offer him the badge. The cowboy wouldn't take it. He just opened the door and went up the stairs to see Dunwood.

"My Lord," Addie said to herself. "I may get that widow's pension a lot sooner than I thought."

11

Slocum's boot heels clomped on the wooden steps, sending a hollow echo through the offices of Dunwood Mining and Team Hauling. The tall man moved uneasily in the new clothes. They rustled and stuck to his skin. He had sweated through the white shirt even though the morning really wasn't that warm. The sight of the tin star had made him jumpy.

"You nervous 'bout somethin'?" Rafferty asked.

Slocum did not reply. He followed Rafferty into a fancy outer office. The walls smelled of fresh cedar wood. It had a rich odor that burned in Slocum's nostrils. The Yankee carpetbaggers had brought a similar stench to Georgia.

"Sit down and wait," Rafferty said.

Slocum's eyes narrowed. "I don't take orders from you."

Rafferty bristled under his duster. His face grew tense at the mouth. Balled fists hung from his sleeves, ready to strike.

"If it's gonna happen, let it come now," Slocum said, never backing down an inch. "What's it gonna be?"

Rafferty smiled, deflating some. "No, not now. Not while we need you. I'll settle this later."

"You do that."

Rafferty glared at him for a second and then spun quickly, disappearing into another office. Slocum had no idea why Rafferty wanted to try him. Maybe the man in the duster just had to be the biggest rooster in the barnyard. Slocum didn't

83

plan on hanging around long enough to let Rafferty have the first swing.

Slocum's green eyes wandered over the office. Was this the place where Dunwood had hidden the gold? Slocum still had a hunch that the gold might not belong to Dunwood. That made it ripe for the taking.

He fixed his gaze on a wall map. A red line had been drawn in from the east and the word "RAILROAD" was written over the line in red capital letters. The track line seemed to be stretching toward Rock Springs.

"Sheriff Hanson?"

Slocum looked around to see Dunwood standing there. The office door was open. Dunwood was a sneaky one. Slocum hadn't heard him coming.

"Come on in, Sheriff."

Slocum winced at the title. He could never be a lawman. He wasn't even sure he could pretend to be one.

Dunwood frowned. "Where's your badge?"

Slocum started toward him. "In Jones's pocket."

"Is something wrong, Hanson?"

"No, not yet."

Dunwood shook his head. "Then what—"

Slocum brushed past him. "We still got talkin' to do."

Slocum entered the office, which had the same smell of wealth. Rafferty stood behind a desk with his thumbs in his belt. He glared at Slocum but the tall man didn't pay him any mind.

"Make yourself comfortable," Dunwood said sarcastically.

Slocum fell into a chair and took off his hat. He had to keep it simple. Too much jawing could result in a mistake that might lead to his undoing.

Dunwood circled around behind the desk. Rafferty kept leaning against the wall. They were an odd team. Rafferty looked like one of those hired guns that came out of Denver. Why didn't Dunwood make him sheriff?

"I suppose you want to discuss salary," Dunwood said.

Slocum shrugged. "Not salary. Why?"

"Why what?" Dunwood asked impatiently.

Slocum gestured with his hand. "Why do you need a sheriff for this place? Hell, you got duster-boy here."

Rafferty came off the wall, pointing a finger at him. "Watch it, Hanson. I won't tolerate no more of that smart mouth."

The tall man kept cool in the chair. "You know somebody jumped that stage out there. This town is rougher than you led me to believe."

"Railroad thugs," Dunwood replied. "But you took care of them. There won't be anything like that again. I assure you—"

Slocum sighed, shaking his head. "Everybody wants to suck up to you smilin' bastards, lyin' to you everywhere you go. I know what I seen, Dunwood. You got trouble here."

Rafferty chortled derisively. "He ain't so tough. Maybe he didn't even take that railroad gang."

"I took 'em," Slocum replied.

"You got lucky," Rafferty scoffed. "Then we caught you."

Slocum catapulted out of the chair. "I ain't listenin' to your mouth no more, Rafferty. Like I said, if you want it to happen, better now than later."

Rafferty's hand dropped, but Slocum already had the Colt out of his holster. Rafferty stared at the bore, which was pointed at his chest. The hammer was back and Slocum's finger was on the trigger.

"That's enough!" Dunwood cried.

Slocum held steady with the Peacemaker. "He's askin' for it, Dunwood. He's gonna get it too, if he don't simmer down."

Dunwood motioned toward the door. "Rafferty, go check on the other men."

"You're makin' a mistake, Mayor," Rafferty said. "This man ain't Brick Hanson. I don't care what he says."

"Go!" Dunwood cried. "Now!"

Rafferty slunk around the desk, moving for the door. Slocum followed him with the barrel of the Peacemaker. Rafferty went out and slammed the door behind him. Slocum turned back to Dunwood with the Colt still in hand.

"There won't be any need for that," Dunwood said.

Slocum kept his hand full of iron. "You talk first and then let me decide if I need it."

"Very well," Dunwood replied calmly. "Sit down and I'll tell you everything you need to know."

Rafferty tore down the stairs, stomping into the street. He stopped abruptly and gazed up at the hotel. The woman. She was in there just waiting to betray the man who called himself

Hanson. She was a whore. Rafferty knew it. She couldn't be a sheriff's wife.

Sweat had broken out on his upper lip. He remembered the curves of the woman when they had pulled her out of the river. The fabric of her dress had clung tightly to her breasts. Rafferty licked his lips. He wouldn't mind having a little bit of the sheriff's wife.

He stormed across the street, climbing the stairs to the second floor of the hotel. She was in there. Waiting for him. He knew she wanted it.

Rafferty balled up his fist and rapped soundly on the door.

Dunwood folded his hands into a steeple and looked over his fingertips at Slocum. "Hanson, if that is your name. . . ."

Dunwood had his doubts too. Why was he playing it out? Why did he need Slocum to be Hanson now? Why didn't he care about the masquerade?

"You don't seem like a stupid man to me. So why don't you tell me what you've figured out so far?"

Slocum lowered the pistol and shrugged. "You're the money man in this town. Ain't much you don't own."

"Very good," Dunwood said. "What else?"

"Mining town," Slocum went on slowly. "You got the mines. You got some kind of hauling business. But that don't explain why you need a sheriff."

Dunwood stood, pacing back and forth. "Did you see the map on the wall in my outer office?"

Slocum nodded. "Railroad. And you said somethin' about railroad thugs. Is that it?"

"Yes," Dunwood replied with a frown, like he hadn't expected his new lawman to be so sharp. "But that's no concern of yours."

"Tell me or I walk," Slocum threatened.

Dunwood sat down again. "It's a complicated matter."

"I'm listenin'."

Dunwood tried to lay it out simply. His mines were going dry. The company hadn't struck a major vein in more than six months. The team hauling business was making more money than the mines. With the arrival of the railroad in Rock Springs, Dunwood's main source of income would dry up alongside the silver digs.

"You been fightin' with the railroad?" Slocum asked.

Dunwood's eyes drifted away. "I'm not at liberty to discuss that."

Slocum felt his gut starting to burn. Rich weasels never wanted to talk about any wrong they had been doing. They wanted to sweep it under the rug or lock it up in a carpetbag.

"We need a sheriff in this town," Dunwood went on. "The citizens of Rock Springs have hopes and dreams. They want those hopes and dreams to be protected by the law."

Slocum shifted uneasily in the chair. "What happened to the last sheriff?"

"An unfortunate accident."

Slocum grimaced. "I bet."

Dunwood sighed impatiently. "Do you want the job or don't you?"

Slocum saw the opening. He had to be smooth about it. If Dunwood suspected that the tall man planned to flee, he might not cooperate.

"You can't keep the railroad out," Slocum said. "And I won't help you try. Is that clear?"

Dunwood smiled, making a conciliatory gesture with his hands. "All I'm asking you to do is protect the little man in Rock Springs. There's not much to it really. You'll see. It's a peaceful town."

Slocum knew that there was no such thing as a peaceful mining town, especially one that was going dry. But he still had his own interests to consider. And that meant working on Dunwood, getting some things out of him.

"I'm waiting for your answer," the mayor insisted.

Slocum leaned forward a little. "Well, I'm all for taking this job. But I got other things that need tendin'."

Dunwood smiled. "Like what?"

"Well, I don't need much, but my wife, well, she's already startin' in on me 'bout where we're gonna live and all."

Dunwood leaned back in his chair. "I see. Go on."

Slocum gestured toward the hotel. "All her fineries were ruined in that coach wreck. She's gonna need a lot of stuff. You know how women are. They need more things than men."

Without hesitation, Dunwood opened a desk drawer and took out a leather pouch. He tossed the pouch onto his desk.

Slocum heard the clinking of gold coins. He knew that sound even through muffled leather.

"Your first month's wages," Dunwood said. "Three hundred dollars. I'll arrange to have your bill paid at the hotel. If you—"

"If I survive," Slocum said. "Then what?"

"The house, just like I promised."

Slocum stood and grabbed the pouch from the desktop. He had no intention of sharing it with his "wife." He'd wait until dark and then get the hell out of Wyoming. Nobody could stop him now.

Dunwood gestured toward the leather bag. "Count it."

Slocum dumped fifteen double eagles into his hands. It was the same gold that had come from the stage coach. Slocum recognized the minting date.

"You'll get that every month if you play your cards right," Dunwood said. "Maybe more."

Slocum gazed at the mayor's pasty face. "And all I got to do is protect the citizens of this town?"

"If you can handle it."

Slocum felt the gold fever. Three hundred a month. He hadn't seen that kind of geetus in a long time.

No, he couldn't do it. He didn't have it in him to be a sheriff, not for one minute. Or so he thought.

"Do we have a deal?" Dunwood asked.

Slocum thought about the rest of the gold that had been in the strongbox. It had to be nearby. If he hung around a little longer . . . no, he couldn't.

"Hanson?"

Grab a horse after dark, ride out, be thankful he had the three hundred. But he couldn't say that to Dunwood. He had to lie convincingly.

"I'm waiting, Sheriff."

Slocum nodded. "Okay."

"Then put on your badge."

The tall man shook his head. "No tin star."

Dunwood scowled at him. "How will everyone know you're the sheriff?"

"They'll know," Slocum replied. "It's a small town. Word will get around. I don't need a badge."

"If you are going to be sheriff—"

Slocum gestured to the window. "The sun will reflect on a tin star. A blind man could tell I was sheriff from a mile away."

"I'm paying you good money to—"

Slocum tossed the bag back on the desk. "We could end it right here."

"No, you said—"

Slocum pointed a finger at him. "Don't lead me on like a green kid, Dunwood. You got a lot of forks in the fire. Stirring the coals is gonna make a lot of sparks in this town. I'd hate to be in the middle when it catches fire."

"You said you would be sheriff."

"Yeah, but not a target. I don't care what you're payin' me, I still got to do things my own way. Understand? *Comprende*? Savvy?"

A curious expression spread over Dunwood's face. "I underestimated you, Hanson. I might be able to use you for other things."

"I told you, I don't want to take on no railroad."

"Things could get hot around here," Dunwood said cautiously.

Slocum picked up the bag of gold again. "It's every man for hisself if the fire gets out of control."

"Protect my people," Dunwood replied. "That's all you have to do."

Slocum tipped his hat in a mocking gesture. "I'll check back with you tomorrow morning."

"See that you do, Hanson. Daily reports, you hear me?"

Slocum turned away and walked off without looking back. He had the money in his hand. Now he had to put it to good use.

Down the stairs, into the street, looking right and left for a livery. He saw that Dunwood owned the stable too. So what? The sheriff had to have a mount. It made sense that he would buy a horse.

Slocum shivered through his shoulders. The word "sheriff" kept ringing in his ears. How the hell had he gotten himself into this mess?

It didn't matter. He just had to get the hell out of Rock Springs. He would go as soon as the sun went down.

At the livery, he found a big-armed man who let him look

over the horses in the stable. Slocum chose a big gray gelding. He asked the man for a price.

"Fifty dollars," the smithy said.

Slocum wondered if his saddle was around somewhere. He asked for the price of tack. The man quoted him another thirty dollars. Slocum decided to take the offer and cut his losses. Leaving town was the most important thing.

"Say," the smith went on. "You wouldn't be the new sheriff would you?"

Slocum hesitated. "Uh, well—"

The smithy extended his hand. "Jonas Brendle," he said with a smile. "Look here, Mr. Dunwood told me to take care of you if you came by. You still want the gray and the saddle, it's yours for the takin'. No charge."

Slocum smiled. "Yeah?"

Brendle waved his hand in the air. "Don't belong to me. I work for Mayor Dunwood, just like you."

Yeah, Slocum thought, but I ain't gonna be working for him much longer.

Brendle squinted at Slocum's chest. "Where's your star?"

"I ain't got it yet," Slocum replied. "Look here, I want to ride my rounds tonight. Can you have that gray ready before sundown?"

"Sure, Sheriff."

Slocum winced again. He had to get away from that word. But he never figured that cruel fate would turn him in another direction entirely.

12

When Addie Hanson heard the knock on the door, she hesitated before she answered. "Yes, who is it?"

"Rafferty, ma'am. I come to check on you."

Addie grimaced. What the hell was Dunwood's right-hand man doing in the hotel? Why would he call on the sheriff's wife?

He wants a little, she thought.

"Mrs. Hanson?"

"Just a minute."

Addie wondered how to play him. She could just send him away, but that wouldn't help her any. After all, if her "husband" didn't live very long in Rock Springs, as her real husband hadn't, she might need Rafferty and Dunwood.

She kept him waiting awhile, affecting the tease the best way she knew. It had to be right, not too obvious, not too subtle. Keep him going even if she wasn't going to let him have the prize.

"Mrs. Hanson?"

"I told you I'll be there in a minute."

After dousing her bosom with perfume, she slipped on her robe and opened the door. Rafferty was hanging there like a horny cowboy. His eyes were sort of glassy, his face was tense. She had seen the look a hundred thousand times when she was whoring. Men just naturally wanted what a woman had. Fate had dealt her a royal flush between her legs.

"You kept me waitin'," Rafferty said.

She frowned at him, feigning displeasure. "My husband isn't here, sir. You can come back another time."

Rafferty grinned uneasily. "What makes you think I come to see your husband? If he *is* your husband."

She started to close the door in his face. Rafferty stopped her. He eased into the hotel room, forcing her to move back.

"When my husband hears of this—"

Rafferty guffawed. "What are you gonna tell him? Huh?"

Her face turned red. "He'll fix your wagon."

Rafferty took off his hat, tossing it on the hook on the back of the door. "Let's you and me have a little talk."

"We have nothing to talk about."

"Come clean, honey," he said, inching closer. "Why don't you tell me who he really is?"

"I don't know what you mean."

"Sure you do," Rafferty went on. "You know as well as I do that cowboy ain't named Brick Hanson."

"How can you be so sure?" she challenged.

Rafferty eased down into the chair, propping up his boots on the edge of the bed. "We got letters from the Kansas City police, honey. They described your husband and he sure as hell don't look like that drifter you hooked up with."

She looked away clutching her robe tightly at her throat. "He's been a little sick."

"You got anythin' that proves he's your husband?"

"He's sharing my bed," she replied.

Rafferty chortled. "Yeah, like he's the first one."

Addie pointed toward the exit. "Leave this room right now or I'll start to scream."

He ignored her threat. "Look here, honey, you're a chippy. I seen a dozen like you come and go in this town. How'd you get a police constable to marry you anyways? He get tired of arrestin' you?"

Addie started for the door. "I won't listen to this. I'm going to get the manager."

Rafferty came out of the chair, grabbing her arm. "You ain't goin' nowhere till I get the truth."

He pushed her back toward the bed. Addie stood there, glaring at him. She wasn't afraid. She was angry.

"You bastard!"

Rafferty laughed again, standing between her and the door. "Where'd you meet the cowboy? Huh? When did y'all decide to steal the strongbox? Or did he run out on you, leavin' you for dead?"

"It was just like he said," Addie replied. "He thought I was dead so he decided to bring the gold back to Rock Springs. You're a fool to think anything else. A stupid fool!"

Rafferty took a step toward her. Addie raised her hand, showing her fingernails. She threatened to scratch out his eyes if he came any closer.

"Just like a cat," Rafferty replied.

"I mean it!"

He shook his head. "Why don't you just tell us the truth? Dunwood will take care of you."

"My husband takes care of me!"

Rafferty gestured at the window. "It's a pretty tough town out there. Hanson may not last any longer than the others."

"He'll kill you when I tell him about this."

"Me? No, it'll be the other way around."

"Get out. Get out now!"

Rafferty shook his head. "I'm not going anywhere. Nope, you're gonna tell me the truth."

Addie turned her back on him. "Go to hell!"

"I plan to," he replied. "Only I'm gonna go to heaven first. And you're gonna go with me."

Addie considered screaming, though she wondered if it would do any good. Where the hell was the cowboy? Was he still talking to Dunwood?

"I'm gonna do somethin' nice for you," Rafferty went on. "Look here. I've got a surprise."

She glanced over her shoulder. Rafferty had unbuttoned his pants. His Johnson was hanging limply through the fly.

"You like it?" he asked.

"I've seen better," she scoffed.

He laughed. "Yeah, in Denver, some of the whores call me 'Dynamite'."

It was her turn to laugh. "Yeah? Well, if you're really dynamite, then you got an awful short fuse."

His face twisted into a hateful scowl. "You bitch. I'm gonna show you what it's like to get topped by a real man."

Rafferty rushed at her. Addie tried to fight him, but his

weight knocked her backwards onto the bed. Rafferty squirmed on top of her, trying to get her legs apart. She could feel his hardness growing.

"Stop it! Stop it!"

Rafferty laughed. "You want it. You know you want it."

Addie screamed at the top of her lungs.

Suddenly the door flew open.

"That's enough, Rafferty."

Slocum stood in the doorway, his green eyes narrow with anger. His Colt was drawn. And he was ready to kill the man in the duster.

13

Rafferty tried to roll off the woman. She squirmed from beneath him, jumping out of the bed. Rafferty fumbled with his fly, trying to get his cock back into his jeans. Slocum kept the pistol pointed at him.

Addie ran to Slocum's side, grabbing him. "Oh, it was terrible. He forced his way in here."

"Son of a bitch," Slocum muttered.

Rafferty stood quickly, buttoning his fly. "You got it all wrong, Sheriff. She invited me in here. Said she wanted it."

"I did not!" Addie cried.

Slocum's finger was tight on the trigger. He considered killing Rafferty right then. The man in the duster sure as hell had it coming.

"Shoot him!" Addie cried. "Gun him down."

Rafferty laughed again. "He don't have the guts."

Slocum eased off on the trigger. As much as he wanted to shoot Rafferty, he knew that it might interfere with his plans. If he killed Dunwood's man, the other hired guns might come after him. And he sure as hell didn't need that, not with his escape plan in full swing.

"Get on out of here!" Slocum said.

"See," Rafferty challenged. "I told you he didn't have the guts."

"Go swing your dick somewhere else!" Addie cried.

Slocum lowered the Peacemaker, but he did not holster

up. He kept the weapon hanging by his side. He wanted to be ready in case Rafferty went for a pistol under that duster.

Rafferty started for the door. "You're in my way," he said.

Slocum stepped aside, moving Addie away. "I don't want to see your face in this hotel as long as I'm here," Slocum told him.

"Fine by me," Rafferty said. "If I'm—"

He turned suddenly, charging Slocum, coming over the top with a hard right hand. Slocum tried to raise the Peacemaker, but the blow caught him on the side of the head. He dropped the gun and fell back against the wall.

Addie lunged at Rafferty, but he backhanded her, sending her to the floor. He came at Slocum again, fists flying. But this time Slocum was ready for him.

The tall man ducked under the blow, sending a right upper-cut into Rafferty's gut. Rafferty grunted and stepped back. Slocum swung his left hand, catching the man squarely on the nose.

Rafferty staggered backward with blood dripping from his nostrils. Slocum started after him. But Rafferty reached into his duster, bringing out a pocket revolver. Slocum had to stop dead in his tracks.

"I ain't afraid to shoot a man," Rafferty said through gnashing teeth.

Slocum stared at the tiny bore of the weapon. It wasn't a big gun, but it was enough to kill him at this range. Rafferty wouldn't miss.

The man in the duster smiled sickly. "Yeah, I've got the gun now. How you want it? In the chest? The head? How 'bout the gut? That's where they say it's the most painful. If you— argh—"

Addie had jumped on Rafferty. She leaped from behind, grabbing his gun hand. When she sank her teeth into the meat of his wrist, he cried out and dropped the pocket revolver.

Slocum got on him again. He grabbed the front of the duster, slapping Rafferty back and forth with the flat of his hand. Rafferty lifted a knee, slamming it toward Slocum's groin.

Slocum flinched at the last moment. The knee hit his thigh. It hurt a little, but not as badly as it would have if he had gotten it in the crotch.

He smashed Rafferty with a fist, knocking him back on the bed. "You're a ball-hitter, huh?"

Rafferty squirmed on the bed, groaning.

"I never cottoned to no ball-hitters."

"I'm gonna kill him!"

Slocum looked back to see a demonic expression on Addie's face. She had picked up the pocket revolver. The barrel was pointed at Rafferty.

"No," Addie said. "I won't kill him. I'll just shoot off his dick. He's gonna be a geldin' when I get through with him."

Rafferty raised his head. "No. Don't let her, Hanson."

Slocum snorted at him. "Why not? You came in here tryin' to force yourself on her."

"She's a whore!" Rafferty moaned.

"That's it," Addie said. "Now he's goin' to get it!"

She thumbed back the hammer of the weapon, taking careful aim.

"No," Rafferty begged. "Don't."

Slocum thought about letting her do it. But he knew it might interfere with his plans. He had to get out of Rock Springs. Rafferty's death might put a burr under somebody's saddle.

"That's enough, woman," he told Addie.

"I'm gonna do it."

Slocum stepped between her and Rafferty. "No. He ain't worth it. Just let it be."

"He's got it comin'."

Slocum held out his hand. "I know. And he's prob'ly gonna get it. But he ain't gonna get it from you."

"I hate him!"

"Come on, Addie. We can't have the sheriff's wife killin' people. Give me the gun."

Addie deflated a little. "Oh, here."

Slocum took the pistol, wondering what would happen to her after he left Rock Springs. "There you go, honey. You won't—"

"Look out!" Addie cried.

Rafferty had come off the bed, charging Slocum again. He grabbed the tall man from behind, squeezing him in a bear hug. Slocum felt the air leaving his lungs. But Rafferty let go as quickly as he had attacked.

Addie had thrown herself on him again, biting his face and

clawing his throat. He spun in a circle, screeching for Slocum to get the woman off him. Slocum just watched as Addie tore up the man in the duster like a female cougar protecting her young.

When Rafferty finally managed to knock her away, Slocum picked up the slack, pistol-whipping him with the pocket revolver. He slapped him out into the hall and then shoved him down the steps. Rafferty rolled into the lobby of the hotel, unconscious from the beating.

"That'll learn him," Slocum muttered.

He went back into the room. Addie threw her arms around him. She sobbed like a schoolgirl. Slocum stroked her hair and told her it was going to be all right. They might have jumped into bed, but a young man appeared at the doorway.

"Sheriff?"

Slocum gazed into the lad's expectant face. "What is it?"

"There's trouble," the boy said. "You got to come."

"I settled the trouble," Slocum replied.

The boy shifted on his feet. "No, sir. It's at the saloon. You got to come now."

Sweat broke out on Slocum's upper lip. He hadn't counted on this. He had been expecting to leave as soon as the sun went down. Now they wanted him to settle some kind of trouble in the saloon.

"Sheriff?" the lad said again. "Are you comin'?"

Slocum hesitated, thinking that he should flee right now.

"Yes," Addie replied. "The sheriff is coming."

Slocum glared at her. "What the. . . ."

She leaned close, whispering in his ear. "You got to do it. For us. For me. I'll do you right when you get back."

If I get back, Slocum thought.

"Hurry, Sheriff," the lad insisted.

Slocum started to follow the boy. He didn't have much choice. Like it or not, he was sheriff of Rock Springs, at least until the sun went down.

14

Slocum followed the messenger down the stairs. Rafferty was still lying on the floor just beyond the last step. Three men in dusters were hovering over him. Slocum hesitated, dropping his hand to the butt of the Colt. He thought he might have to try them all.

"What'd you do to him?" asked Hud Jones.

Slocum shrugged. "He tripped and fell down the stairs."

Jones laughed. "Don't that beat all."

The others laughed too. They knew Slocum had beaten the tar out of Rafferty but they didn't seem to care. They showed all the loyalty of hired guns, Slocum thought. He couldn't get out of Rock Springs soon enough.

Slocum and the boy moved around Rafferty, heading for the door. When they were outside, the kid wanted to run. Slocum grabbed his arm and stopped him. There wasn't any rush to get to the source of the trouble.

"What's wrong, Sheriff?" the kid asked.

Slocum lifted his eyes to the saloon, which seemed calm enough. "What's goin' on over there, boy?"

A fearful expression spread over the boy's face. "Rooster Bateman has come into town, Sheriff."

Slocum grimaced painfully at the use of his new title.

"Hey, Sheriff, where's your badge?"

Slocum glared at the kid. "Never you mind. Tell me about this Bateman."

"Works his own mine up yonder," the boy replied. "But every time he comes to town, he breaks up the saloon and then kills a few people. He was the one what killed our last sheriff."

The tall man sighed, tipping back his hat. Why the hell didn't Dunwood's men handle something like this? Because they didn't care about the people of Rock Springs, Slocum told himself. There was a line between Dunwood and the local populace. The duster men weren't going to cross that line unless they were ordered to do it.

"Better hurry, Sheriff," the kid pleaded.

Slocum stared across the street. "Who does Bateman ride with?"

"He's got brothers that help him work the claim."

"How many?"

The kid shrugged. "Don't know exactly. Sometimes there's two, sometimes three. Depends on—"

"How many are over there now?" Slocum asked.

"I don't know, Sheriff. Somebody just told me to come get you. I ran as fast as I could."

"I want you to get gone," Slocum said.

The kid started to bolt.

"No, wait. Where's a gunsmith in this town?"

The boy pointed up the street. "In the first alley. A man named Simm. He's there now, I think."

"Get gone. And tell the man at the general store I said to give you a bag of horehound candy."

The kid smiled, revealing brown, stumpy teeth. "I'd rather have chewin' tobacco."

"Get gone!"

Slocum began to walk up the dirty street, keeping his sidelong gaze trained on the saloon. When he passed by the double swinging doors, he could hear somebody talking loudly. He wondered if Rooster Bateman was working up to his reputed meanness. There was only one sure way to stop a man running wild—shoot him.

The gunsmith's shop was a small hovel in the shadows of an alley. The place smelled of gun oil and black powder. Slocum found a gray-haired man slumped over a Colt cylinder.

He looked up at Slocum with glassy eyes. "Help you?"

Slocum nodded. "Hanson's the name," he lied. "Dunwood hired me."

The gunsmith nodded back. "The new sheriff. When'd you get in?"

"Yesterday."

"And you're still alive. Congratulations. Name's Jimmy Simm. They call me Simm. Used to call me Mad Dog in my younger days. You want a shot of whiskey?"

Slocum squinted at the little man. "I reckon." A belt might take the edge off things. And he still needed some information.

Simm poured two blasts of some clear liquid. It burned like horse liniment. But that didn't stop Slocum from asking for a second shot.

"Look here, Simm. What's all this about Rooster Bateman?"

Simm made a clicking noise and shook his head. "Bad one there."

"Is it true he kills people every time he comes to town?"

"That'd be right," Simm replied.

"Can't allow that," Slocum said. "What you got that'll stop him?"

Simm held up a finger. "Scatter-gun. Ten gauge. You could blow a hole in him the size of Cheyenne."

"Mind if I borrow it?"

Simm leaped from his workbench like a leprechaun. He disappeared into a dark back room and came out with a long shotgun. Slocum figured this blunderbuss would stop anything short of a grizzly.

Simm slid two brass cartridges into the weapon. "Special loads," he said. "Buckshot and small nails. Get a good spray. It takes out whatever's in front of you and stings whatever's on the side."

Slocum thought that sounded good.

Simm pointed to his firearm. "Let me look at your pistol. If you're goin' after Bateman, you'll want everythin' to work."

Slocum handed him the Peacemaker. Simm turned the cylinder. He listened to the clicking of the mechanism.

"Good," he said to the tall man. "My work."

Slocum remembered that he had gotten the pistol from the man he killed at the river. "Who'd you—"

"One of those riders who works for Dunwood," Simm replied.

If that was true, Slocum thought, then it had been Dunwood's men who robbed the stage. Maybe that was why Rafferty hated Slocum. The lanky rebel drifter had taken out some of Rafferty's men. Why didn't they just kill him? Did Dunwood really need a sucker to be sheriff that badly?

Simm handed him the weapon. "You should do all right."

"Are there any whores at the saloon?" Slocum asked.

Simm laughed. "Hell, I don't know. I'm too old for that. There used to be a girl, but I don't know if she's still there."

Slocum took the shotgun from him. "Much obliged, sir."

Simm thrust a handful of shells at him. "Extras."

"I'll bring it back when I'm done."

Simm waved him off. "Keep it. I'll soak Dunwood with the bill. Everybody in town has the word to take care of you."

Slocum eyed the gray man, wondering how much anyone in this town could be trusted. "You got anythin' to say 'bout Dunwood?"

"He puts hisself first," the gunsmith replied. "He'll pay you good, but he'd push his own mother into the flames to escape the fire. And if you say I said that, I'll call you a liar."

Slocum thanked him and went out into the alley. His heart was pumping. He had killed a lot of men, but he had never arrested one. What the hell did the citizens of Rock Springs expect anyway?

"Better get it done."

He started across the street to face Rooster Bateman.

Rafferty stirred on the floor of the hotel lobby. He focused on his men hovering over him. When he remembered what had happened, he made a growling noise and sat up.

"You okay?" asked Hud Jones.

Rafferty scowled at him. "Get me on my feet."

They lifted him until he stood on wobbly legs. The duster men were all trying to keep from smiling. They hated Rafferty. It had given them pleasure to see the sheriff best their bullying boss.

Rafferty turned to shout up the stairs. "I'm gonna fix you, Hanson. You hear me! I'm goin' to see Dunwood right now. I'm gonna fix you good!"

In her room, Addie Hanson heard the threat. She had been thinking about a widow's pension. Now that she was starting to like the tall cowboy, she wasn't sure she wanted to draw it.

Slocum cautiously approached the front door of the saloon. The street was empty, though Slocum could feel the eyes peering at him from half-opened windows and cracked doors. Nobody wanted to get directly in the line of fire.

Holding the scatter-gun across his belly, he eased to the edge of the entrance, listening for signs of trouble. It was quiet inside. Then the loud voice came bellowing out of the shadows.

"Ain't nobody gonna stop me from doin' what I want," the voice proclaimed. "I'm Rooster Bateman and I'm the toughest son of a bitch in Wyomin'!"

Slocum thumbed back the twin hammers of the ten gauge. He figured Bateman was somewhere near the bar, wherever that was. Something crashed in the saloon. Breaking glass seemed to scatter. Bateman was boiling.

"Sons of bitches," he cried. "I'm gonna kill a son of a bitch. Who wants to die first?"

A few drunks burst out of the saloon, running into the street to escape the madman. They didn't even notice Slocum standing there with the shotgun. He kept waiting, listening to the scuffle of feet on wood.

Inside, somebody started to beg for his life. There were slapping noises. A man flew through the double doors, rolling into the street.

Slocum shook his head. He had never liked bullies. Maybe it was better if he *didn't* try to arrest this crazy.

"I want me a drink!" Bateman cried. "Where's that bottle? I'm gonna have to kill me a bartender."

Pistol fire erupted inside. Slocum heard more breaking glass. He counted six shots and then the place was quiet again.

Rooster was holding an unloaded pistol now. Slocum had to take his chances. He shouldered through the double doors and peered into the shadows.

Bateman had his back to the door. He spun quickly to face Slocum. Whiskey ran down his greasy beard onto his chest. He was big, ugly, and toothless, dressed like a mountain man.

Bateman grinned at Slocum. "Well, if it ain't the sheriff. The new sheriff. I been hankerin' to kill me a lawman all day. I—"

Slocum lifted the shotgun and pulled both triggers. The noise of the discharge deafened him. Smoke filled the air. He couldn't see for a moment.

When the air had cleared a little, he detected Rooster Bateman's form against the bar. The big man was twitching. His hands flailed at the air like a drowning man.

"Lordy," Bateman said. "I been shot. I. . . ."

Slocum took a couple of steps toward the fallen outlaw. Bateman had a bloody cavity in his chest. The meat from the hole had splattered all over the bar and the wall behind the bar. He died in a few seconds.

Something rustled to Slocum's left. He wheeled quickly, dropping the scatter-gun, coming up with his Colt. A man who resembled Bateman staggered toward him. Blood poured from his face. He had small nails imbedded in his flesh, the result of the side-spray by Simm's special load.

The man started to lift a rusty Remington .44. Slocum had to shoot him in the chest with the Peacemaker. He died more slowly than his brother.

Brothers, Slocum thought. What had the kid said? Sometimes two, sometimes three.

A third pistol exploded behind Slocum. Slugs whizzed over his head. He hit the deck, rolling over to face the direction of the gunfire. The shots had come from the window. He saw the shadow jump away to hide behind the outer wall of the saloon.

Slocum marked the man's position. The third Bateman fired through the window again. He screamed something about avenging his brothers.

Slocum crawled toward the scatter-gun. He dug into his pockets, coming up with two more of the brass shells. He loaded the weapon as the third brother emptied his pistol through the window.

"Ain't no sheriff gonna stop us Batemans!" he cried.

Slocum lifted the scatter-gun, aiming at the wall. "Don't bet on it, asshole."

He tripped both triggers. The shotgun erupted again. When the smoke cleared, Slocum saw the hole in the wall.

The last Bateman brother appeared in the casement of the window. Slocum began to reload. But he did not need the shotgun now. Bateman slumped over the sill and lay there, dying. Part of his throat had disappeared so he made horrible sounds until the last ember of life had faded.

Slocum put the shells into the scatter-gun. He turned in a slow arc, waiting for another attack. The double doors flew open. Two men rushed in from the street.

He leveled the shotgun at Dunwood and Rafferty. Rafferty had drawn his gun. Slocum pointed the barrels at the duster man's chest.

"No need for that," Dunwood said.

Rafferty holstered up the weapon. "I'll be damned."

Slocum held steady with the hand-cannon. "It had to be done."

"Surely," Dunwood replied. "Good job, Hanson. These men have been a thorn in the side of this town for as long as anyone can remember."

Rafferty scoffed, "Aw, we coulda taken 'em."

"Yeah, but you didn't," Slocum replied.

There was no challenge from Rafferty. He was still bruised and bloodied from the beating Slocum had given him. Maybe he would back off for the time being.

Dunwood began to move around, directing things. "Get these bodies into the street," he told Rafferty. "And draw a crowd. There has to be a speech on an occasion like this."

Slocum glared at the mayor. "I ain't one for speechifyin'."

"Don't worry," Dunwood told him. "I'll do all the talking."

Slocum watched as the bodies were dragged in front of the saloon. He wondered if there were any more Batemans around. For some unknown reason, he felt a little badly about killing all three of them, though they probably hadn't amounted to much more than trouble all their lives.

When the corpses were in place and the crowd was drawn, Dunwood led Slocum outside. The gawkers eyed the new sheriff as if he were a two-headed rattler. Was he *really* the one who had ended the notorious careers of the Batemans?

"Ladies and gentlemen of Rock Springs," Dunwood started. "I give you your new sheriff, Brick Hanson, formerly of the Kansas City police!"

The citizens applauded mildly. They had seen killings before. A hanging would have gotten a better reaction out of them, but Slocum had cheated the gallows with the scatter-gun.

"Sheriff Hanson—"

At least the mayor wasn't using Slocum's real name with the title.

"—has sworn to protect you from the likes of the Bateman brothers, who are now dispatched to their just reward!"

Another round of clapping. They jockeyed to get a look at the hole in Rooster Bateman's chest. Then they gaped at the sight of the big shotgun on Slocum's hip.

"We will protect you," Dunwood went on, "from the likes of the Batemans, from anyone who would harm you, including those thugs from the railroad!"

No reaction to the mention of the railroad. Did Dunwood really think he was going to stop the tracks from coming in? He was a fool.

The mayor went on talking, but everyone paid more attention to the bodies. They swarmed like ants, threatening to tear the meat right from the carcasses. Slocum felt trapped. But he knew the darkness would free him. All he could do was wait for sundown.

15

Slocum pushed through the crowd, avoiding their faces, fleeing back to the privacy of the hotel. Sheriffing had made him sick to his stomach. The air stank of burnt powder and open wounds. It reminded him of battle, when he had worn the uniform of the gray. He had sworn he would never wear another uniform, but now they had all seen him. They knew he was a lawman even if he wasn't wearing a badge.

"He killed the Batemans."

"He's as tough as Dunwood said."

"Not like that last sheriff."

Their voices faded behind him. He entered the lobby of the hotel where the manager looked concerned. Slocum stomped past him, climbing the stairs.

The woman was waiting for him. She threw her arms around his shoulders, kissing him all over his face. He started to push her away, but realized that he couldn't stop. They groped and grabbed, trying to get naked.

Addie worked his Johnson free of his fly. She fell back on the bed, accepting him, writhing on her back. Slocum plunged in, driving home until he released deep within her.

Slocum rolled off, trying to catch his breath. Addie nuzzled into his chest. He was going to miss her when he left Rock Springs. She'd be one to think about on the dark, lonely nights of the trail—a trail that looked pretty good in the eyes of a bogus lawman.

"You hungry?" she asked.

Slocum nodded. "Yeah."

Addie put on her robe and went downstairs. She returned with fried chicken, biscuits, and gravy. Slocum ate heartily. He wanted to have his strength for the trail.

She also had a bottle, so they drank a couple of shots. Slocum closed his eyes, but the woman wouldn't let him sleep. She jostled around, shaking the headboard and the springs.

"Be still," he told her.

He had to sleep a little. When he got going, he wanted to be able to ride a full day before he stopped. This time, he'd double back to the east, away from the mountains. When he hit level ground, he could head for Missouri or Oklahoma. There weren't many posters on him back that way.

"Look here, cowboy," Addie said.

Slocum opened his eyes. He saw the crack of her ass. She was on all fours, clinging to the foot of the bed, wiggling her backside at him.

"Like a stallion and a mare," she said. "I had a boy from Baltimore who liked it like this."

He had to oblige her. They bounced around until he collapsed on her back. Addie squirmed from beneath him, nuzzling in again. This time she wanted to talk.

"What do you know about the gold?" she asked.

Slocum's eyes popped open. "What?"

"The gold you were trying to steal," she replied. "What happened to it?"

He sighed. "Dunwood has it in his office."

What would it hurt to tell her? He was riding out anyway. It might even work to her advantage if she could spark the old mayor.

"Whose gold is it?" Addie said softly.

"I don't know. I think it was some of Dunwood's hired guns who attacked the stage. I think he deliberately stole the gold."

She squinted at him. "Then why would he keep you on as sheriff?"

"Somebody else to cover him when the bullets start flying."

Addie propped herself on an elbow and looked down into his face. "Let's try to steal back the gold."

He chortled. "Be my guest."

She shook him. "You can do it. You're tough. Look at the way you took out those stage robbers."

"Luck."

"You've got more than luck, honey."

He didn't plan to stay around and push his luck.

"No gold," he told her.

She pouted, looking away. "Did Dunwood give you an advance on your salary?" she asked.

Slocum shook his head. "No. He didn't have it on him."

Her hand came up with the leather pouch that Dunwood had given him. "Then what's this?"

Somehow it didn't surprise Slocum that she had picked his pocket. "You caught me."

"I'm taking it," she said, trying to roll off the bed.

He caught her and pulled her back. "Half and half. We're partners ain't we? I'll share, but you ain't takin' it all."

She held the purse against her bosom. "I've got it coming. I rode all the way out here to this godforsaken place. I'm due."

He snatched the pouch away from her. "You get one double eagle. And don't spend it all in one place."

"You're mean to me."

"Why not? We're married."

She tucked the double eagle into her bosom, patting it for safekeeping. Slocum dropped the pouch into his boot and then put the boot under his pillow. He warned her not to touch the boot.

"What about the house?" she asked.

"It'll come later."

She leaned over, putting her head on his chest. "You aren't going to leave are you? I mean, I don't know what I'd do without you."

"You'd probably manage," he replied.

She sighed. "All that gold."

The thought of the double eagles kept the tall man from closing his eyes. All that loot, going to waste on a carpetbagger like Dunwood. A man could declare himself a king down in Mexico if he had that much money.

"Maybe I could get close to him," Addie went on. "Dunwood, I mean. Or maybe Rafferty."

Slocum found himself growing jealous. "You stay away from Rafferty."

"He might lead us to the gold if I play him right," Addie said. "I mean, he wants it."

Slocum bristled but he didn't say another word. What did it matter if Addie tried to feather her own nest after he was gone? She had a right. And he really didn't care about her. He just hated Rafferty.

"You want to do it again?" she asked.

Slocum grunted. "No."

"I need another shot."

She got out of bed to pour the hooch. Slocum closed his eyes, trying to forget about the gold. It was there in the office, probably not even locked up in a closet or a safe. Dunwood had the duster riders to protect it.

He shook off the ill feeling. It was best to get out of Wyoming. He had been unlucky in the cursed territory.

Slocum stiffened when the loud knocking shook the door to the room. "What now? We gonna hang someone?"

"Sheriff?"

He hated that word. "Go away, I'm sleepin'."

"Sheriff Hanson?"

Slocum frowned. He did not recognize the voice. The man kept insisting that Slocum open the door.

"I'm Andrew Gable of the Wyoming Railroad Line," the intruder called from the hall. "I need to see you immediately."

Slocum's mouth went dry. He hadn't figured on the railroad people showing up so soon. News of his recent appointment had gotten around.

"Sheriff Hanson, please. This is a matter of utmost importance. I need to speak with you at once."

Addie gave him a quizzical look. "Railroad man?"

Slocum sighed. "I can't explain it now. Let him in."

He stood, buttoning his fly, straightening his shirt.

Addie let in the visitor, a blond man in a dark suit. Slocum knew at once that Andrew Gable was a Yankee. He had to be from the northeast. Nobody wore a suit like that once they were west of the Mississippi.

"I'm Andrew Gable," he said in a deep voice, extending his hand.

He was handsome enough to attract Addie's attention. "Why, don't you have the prettiest blue eyes."

Slocum's eyes grew narrow. "Why don't you go rustle us up some more grub?" he said bluntly. "And some coffee."

Addie reluctantly closed her robe and started for the stairs. Slocum closed the door behind her. He turned to face the Yankee. At least Gable seemed to have more breeding than most carpetbaggers.

"Sheriff Hanson, I wish to report a missing strongbox full of gold."

Slocum tried not to show his surprise. So the gold had been stolen from the railroad men, not stolen by them. Slocum figured it wasn't any of his business, though, not with his mount awaiting him in the livery.

"There was a strongbox coming here by stage," Gable went on. "We were shipping our payroll on that stage. The company assured us that there would be plenty of guards on the coach. I understand that you yourself were aboard the coach when it was attacked."

Slocum nodded, wondering how much of the real truth was known by Gable. The railroad man might suspect that Dunwood had been behind the robbery. Had he heard that the sheriff's salary was being paid by the same man?

"Did you find the gold?" Gable asked.

"No," Slocum replied calmly. "I did manage to escape with my life. And I took a few of 'em with me. But I never saw the gold again after it was loaded on top of the stage."

Gable shook a piece of paper at him. "I'm offering a five hundred dollar reward for the return of that chest."

Slocum eyed the dapper railroad man. He wondered if Gable was trying to pull him into some kind of trap. Maybe Gable wanted to use him like Dunwood.

"Lemme ask you something," Slocum started. "How come you didn't bring that payroll to your men on the same tracks you're buildin'?"

Gable sighed and shook his head. "That's what we were doing. But our trains have been hit three times by robbers. We thought we could get away with shipping the payroll by stage, but someone must have found out about it."

"Any ideas about who?"

Gable glanced sideways at him. "There are certain men in this area who do not want the railroad to get to Rock Springs."

"What can I do about it?"

"Do the right thing, Sheriff. I don't care who is paying you, you still have to uphold the law."

"I reckon."

What difference did it make? He was leaving. He would have promised the devil his soul to get out of Wyoming.

Gable reached into his coat pocket, taking out more papers. "I have the deeds and the papers for the right of way. Nothing can stop us from coming in here with this railroad. We're only two months away from completing the line. We want to be finished before winter."

"Should be plenty of time," Slocum replied. "You asked for any help from the marshal or the army?"

Gable nodded. "But the marshal is up north in a range war and the army was supposed to send a man who never arrived."

The young lieutenant had died in the stage crash. Slocum told the man as much. Gable said he would send for another army advisor, but until then, the sheriff had a job to do.

"Just one thing," Slocum said. "How much gold was in that strongbox?"

"Five thousand dollars," Gable replied. "I know that's a lot, but some of it was to go for payment of these deeds."

Five thousand in gold coins. Slocum had a memory of that vivid reflection. And he had a good idea where all that geetus was hiding.

"Dunwood won't stop this railroad," Gable said. "There'll be more gold and more tracks."

"I'll see what I can do," Slocum replied.

Gable extended his hand. "Thank you."

Slocum shook his hand and then opened the door. Gable hesitated in the hallway. He looked back at Slocum.

"What?" the tall man asked.

"Do the right thing, Sheriff."

Slocum closed the door. He wasn't thinking about the right thing. He was thinking about a chest full of gold.

16

When Addie Hanson came back to the room, she was carrying a tray with coffee and cake. "Where's the railroad boy?" she asked.

"He left."

"What did he want?"

Slocum grunted. "Nothin'."

Addie put the tray on the dresser. "Want some coffee?"

"No."

"It's yellow cake. Made with real butter."

He shook his head. "Maybe later."

His hands were behind his head on the pillow. He had been looking at the ceiling for a long time. The gold sickness had him. He wanted it to pass so he could get out of town.

"It's the gold, isn't it?" she asked.

Slocum nodded. "Yep."

"What happened?"

"Dunwood stole it from the railroad," Slocum replied. "He's tryin' to keep the railroad out of here. He's goin' to lose his team haulin' business when the train gets into Rock Springs."

She fell next to him on the bed. "I knew it was something like that. Let's steal the gold, honey."

"How would we get it out of here?"

She leaned back, looking at the ceiling herself. "Well, we could . . . I don't know. I guess we could . . . hell!"

"It ain't that easy to carry a bunch of gold."

"I know!" She sat up. "We could steal it, hide it, and then go about our business until nobody was looking. Bang! We dig it up and leave. I'll say that I don't like my dear husband bein' a lawman."

He thought about it. The plan might work. If they were going to take the strongbox, they had to stash it somewhere. They would never get away on horseback. Slocum had already failed once. They'd surely hang him the second time.

"I wonder how much is in there?" she asked.

Slocum didn't tell her. If she knew, she would keep nagging him and he might never talk himself out of trying for the jackpot. Five thousand. Slocum, Mexican *padrone*. He could buy a *rancho* with that much money.

He closed his eyes. When he opened them again, the shadows were longer and the woman snored beside him. He had been asleep all afternoon. He felt rested, ready to go.

Rising, he strapped on his Peacemaker and eased out the door with his hat and boots in hand. He took the money pouch from his boot and held it for a moment. There was so much more gold where that had come from.

The heft of the pouch made his mouth water. He remembered that yellow sheen so well. A whole chest full of double eagles. Five thousand? There had to be more than that. But why would Gable lie?

Slocum couldn't bring himself to leave just yet. He had to make a try for the gold, or at least a scouting run. If he didn't take it all, he could at least fill the pouch again, maybe stack up a few coins in his saddle bags.

"Damn."

He pulled on his boots and headed for the stairs that led to the roof. From his high vantage point, he could see the dark windows of Dunwood's office. There had to be a back way into the place. And if he got caught, he could say he was the sheriff just making his rounds.

Slocum shivered. He was close to calling himself sheriff. Was that what that gold did to a man?

He had to have a look.

When he came back down into the hall, Addie was waiting for him with the door ajar. She caught him trying to sneak by. He startled when she jumped out of the shadows.

"You tryin' to scare me to death, woman?"

She grinned from ear to ear. "You're gonna do it!"

"Shh!"

"No, I can help. Let me help."

He pointed into the room. "Stay here. If I come up with anything, I'll let you know."

She kissed him on the cheek. "Just think. We'll be so happy. You sure you don't want me to help?"

"I said so, didn't I?"

He hurried down the stairs, emerging on the street. It was almost dusk. Slocum could smell the cooking fires. He crossed the street, heading for the alley that led behind Dunwood's building.

Just a quick glance before he left town. What would it hurt? He might never get a chance for another swindle like this one.

When he reached the back alley, he looked up at the rear windows of the office. "Damn."

Lights were burning in the windows. Slocum saw shadows on the wall. He drew closer to the wall. There were stacked wooden crates below the window. Slocum climbed slowly until he was within earshot. Rafferty was talking in a hostile voice. He mentioned the sheriff.

Dunwood's voice rose in the still air. "How many times do I have to tell you that we need Hanson?"

"For what?" Rafferty insisted.

Dunwood sighed. "As the sheriff said, we've got our forks in a lot of fires. If things get out of hand, we're going to need to blame them on somebody. Do you understand what I'm saying?"

"No!"

"Then let me make it clear enough for an idiot. We can blame everything on Hanson if anything goes wrong. Why do you think I hired some thick-headed Kansas City constable? He thinks he's going to roust drunks and shoot men like that animal he killed today."

"I still don't get it," Rafferty replied.

"A sucker, a dupe, a tinhorn."

"Oh. Oooh! I got it. We set him up in case the real law tries to get in our way."

No chance, Slocum thought. He wasn't going to take the fall for anyone. Forget about the gold. He had a real reason to vamoose now.

"Stay out of it with Hanson," Dunwood said. "We need him alive."

"I don't know, Mayor. He doesn't look like any K.C. cop I ever saw. I think he's smarter'n that."

A low, impatient growl escaped from Dunwood's throat. "Don't you see, if he is an impostor, then all the better. One more thing to hang on him. We hang the woman too."

"No," Rafferty said. "I want her for myself."

"Whatever. Now, help me count this. Where was I? Eight thousand sixty—"

Eight thousand! Had Gable been lying too? Who really had a right to all that gold?

Slocum couldn't dwell on such things. He eased himself off the crates and stole quickly back to the street. Hesitating for a moment, he gazed toward the hotel. Maybe he should warn the woman. No, she'd be all right, better off without him. By the time she figured it out, somebody else would be there to take care of her. Slocum sure hoped that she wouldn't go with Rafferty.

Slocum started for the livery. He saw that the light was burning in the general store. He stopped there, buying some jerky, a loaf of bread, and a bottle of whiskey. He told the store owner that he was going to be up all night, guarding the town from would-be outlaws. The storekeeper gladly gave him anything he wanted from the full shelves.

As he made his way to the stable, Slocum thought about the shotgun he had left in the hotel room. He wanted the weapon, but he didn't want to face the woman again. Best just to go on. He hadn't earned the scatter-gun anyway. Addie could give it back to the gunsmith.

The liveryman was glad to see him. He had the gray saddled and ready to ride. Slocum wondered what would happen to the man after Dunwood found out that the new sheriff had run. He supposed that the mayor would make life miserable for everyone in Rock Springs. What did Slocum care? He wouldn't be there to see it happen.

"I heard them Batemans have cousins," the liveryman said.

Slocum shrugged. "I ain't scared of 'em."

"Sheriff?"

Slocum hoped that would be the last time he heard that word directed at him. "Yeah?"

"I just want to shake your hand, sir. Those Bateman boys were always stiffing me when I worked on their horses' shoes. I'm glad they're gone. A lot of us are. You did a good job."

Slocum reluctantly shook hands with him. "Killin' ain't much, boy. You remember that if it gets rough around here."

"Aw, we got you now, Sheriff."

That damned word!

"You'll protect Rock Springs."

Slocum guided the gray out the front door. He wanted everyone to see that the sheriff was on duty. Lifting himself into the saddle, he started to amble down the darkening street. Nosy eyes were peering from behind curtains and shades. He rode past the mining offices.

"Sheriff Hanson!"

He looked up to see Dunwood staring from a window. Slocum's heart began to pound. What if the mayor figured out that he was running?

"Where are you going?" Dunwood asked.

Slocum tipped back his hat, trying to act cool and collected. "Just ridin' on my night rounds, Mayor. Thought I'd let everyone see me goin' up and down. Maybe take a circle around the place. Unless you don't want me to."

"No," Dunwood called. "That's a good idea. Check back with me in an hour. All right?"

"Sure."

An hour. That wasn't much time. But it had to be enough. Slocum waved to Dunwood and urged the horse into a walk.

He didn't look back, but he knew Dunwood was watching him. Slocum went down to the other end of town, turned around and made a second pass under the window. Dunwood was still there, spying from behind a moving curtain.

Slocum repeated the walking routine three more times until the lights went out in the office. Then he spurred the gray toward the east, heading for the blackness beyond the town. He figured they would come after him right away. His only chance was to outrun them.

17

Slocum rode hard to the east, following the main road. The gray was big, fast, strong, and ready to fly. Slocum gave the animal its head, barreling back toward the river.

He followed the arc, coming back on the stream from the bend in the trail. Something told him to turn north. He could follow the water for a while and then throw off the trackers. He was sure that one of Rafferty's boys would know how to track. They'd be close on his tail for a while.

Leaving the gold was the right thing, he told himself. The combination of the woman and the money could be dangerous. He'd find a whore up the way if he got too anxious.

Lead them north, circle back to the south, go on into Colorado. Even if they did stay with him till the territorial border, they'd probably quit once he crossed over.

Hell, they might not even follow him. Dunwood could always find another sucker. Slocum didn't have to take the big fall for the rich man's wrongs.

The gray was steady until Slocum was through the turn. Then the animal slowed and snorted some. Slocum's stomach churned when he saw the torches gliding toward him. The riders seemed to appear out of nowhere.

They all carried torches, all seven of them. They formed a circle around Slocum. Nobody seemed to be holding a weapon. Slocum kept his own hands in plain sight. One sudden move could get him killed by seven slugs.

As they neared the river, the horses had to stop. The ring stayed tight on the tall man. One of the riders slid in close to him. He wasn't dressed in a duster, like Dunwood's boys always wore.

"You can keep your guns," the man said. "But you better not try to use them. Savvy?"

"Savvy. Where are we goin'?"

"North. Hyah!"

They turned north, driving along the banks of the river. When they had gone a couple of miles, they crossed the stream and headed northeast. Slocum kept watching them, waiting and wondering what they wanted.

If they weren't Dunwood's men, then who the hell were they? What did they want with Slocum? They didn't want him dead, at least not yet.

On a stretch of level ground, one of the riders went out ahead, leading the way with the torch. Slocum focused on the horizon. He could see more lights burning in the distance. Then he heard the steam hissing of a locomotive engine. Railroad tracks lay ahead.

"Gable," he said to himself.

They reined up next to a lighted boxcar. Slocum had to dismount. The seven riders urged him toward the entrance to the boxcar.

"I'll take your hog leg now," said the leader.

Slocum gave up his weapon. What else could he do with seven guns in his face? There wouldn't be any escaping this trap unless someone got really careless.

When he entered the ornately furnished traveling car, he saw Gable sitting in a padded chair. The blond man nodded at him. Slocum nodded back. They stared at each other for a moment.

"What will it be?" Gable asked.

Slocum shrugged nonchalantly. "I don't know what you're sayin'."

"You were leaving town," Gable went on. "Why?"

"Sheriffin' didn't work out."

Gable's blue eyes narrowed. "Your name is John Slocum. You aren't a sheriff, you have never been a sheriff."

The tall man's body went slack. "How do you know?"

"You had some trouble in Cheyenne, in a whorehouse. Didn't you?"

"Maybe."

Gable smiled triumphantly. "You blinded a man and then you left on the stage for Rock Springs. You were hired to ride shotgun."

Slocum chortled. "You know an awful lot about me."

"Why were you running out on the Hanson woman?"

Slocum tipped back his hat and shook his head. "I don't know. I guess marriage don't agree with me."

Gable gestured toward a chair. "Sit down. This may be a long night."

Slocum eased back into a wooden seat. "I ain't got much to say, Gable. And I ain't done nothin' wrong."

"Who has the gold?"

What could it hurt to tell him the truth?

"Dunwood," Slocum replied. "He's got it all."

"Are you sure?"

Slocum figured he was bargaining for his life. He took out the leather pouch and dropped it on the table. Gable examined the gold coins closely.

"Yes," the Yankee muttered. "Same minting date. What were you going to do with these?"

"Leave town. Get the hell away from all this. Railroad on one side, Dunwood on the other."

Gable stood up, seething with rage, and began to pace the floor. "Damn it all. I knew he was behind that robbery."

Slocum grimaced at the rich man. "Why don't you just go to the marshal? You got the deeds. The law's on your side."

"The law is a tender matter out here," Gable replied.

"Then ride in with your boys. Clean out the nest."

Gable eyed him cautiously. "I don't detect any trace of loyalty in your voice. I thought you had thrown in with Dunwood."

"Got caught in the current," Slocum replied. "And I'm ready to swim on downstream. Ain't none of this no never mind for me."

Gable's face seemed to brighten. "That's it. You're the one who can help me. If you've no loyalty to Dunwood—"

"No loyalty to you, either," Slocum replied.

Gable leaned forward on the desk. "You can get back that gold for me."

"Ride in with your boys. Take it."

"It's not that simple," Gable said, sighing. "My company doesn't want to resort to those tactics."

"You know that Dunwood is blamin' you for the robbin'," Slocum offered. "He's tryin' to stir up the citizens."

Gable did not reply. Instead, he took a bottle from a cabinet on the wall and poured two drinks. He handed Slocum a glass full of a glowing brown liquid.

"Have you ever had brandy, Mr. Slocum?"

Well, at least he wasn't calling him sheriff.

Slocum drained the glass, wiping his mouth with the back of his hand. It was smooth and sweet. Gable offered him another blast. Slocum declined. He wanted his head to be clear.

"You can go back to Rock Springs in one of two ways," Gable said, with an unfriendly smile. "My boys can escort you in and tell Dunwood that you were trying to escape. Or, you can go back there and find my gold and bring it to me. That's the only thing that can get you off the hook."

Slocum thought about it for a moment. If Dunwood found out he was leaving, there could be an early hanging in town. If he went back now, no one would even know he had left.

"All right," Slocum said. "I'll go back."

"And you'll return my gold to me?"

The big man exhaled tiredly. "No guarantees."

"But you'll try?"

Slocum eyed the smooth Yankee with contempt. "What about me? Who's gonna watch my back?"

"We'll be watching," Gable threatened. "If you try to leave town again, we'll stop you."

"I still don't see why you need me to do this."

"Simple. If you return the gold, we don't have to fight with Dunwood. And there's no delay in the signing of the right of way and the deeds. You're an important man, John Slocum."

Slocum sat up straighter. "If I'm so important, then tell me what's in this for me?"

"You keep the gold in this pouch—and your life."

How could he turn it down?

"Deal," Slocum said.

Gable passed him the pouch. At least he had some of his money. But that damned gold was continuing to be a problem.

"Don't disappoint me," Gable called.

Slocum cleared his throat and spat phlegm on the plush carpet of the boxcar. "Kiss my ass, Yankee."

He grinned as he emerged outside. The railroad men were happy to escort him back to the edge of town. Then they left him to ride in by himself.

When he neared the offices of Dunwood Mining, Slocum saw that Rafferty and his men were ready to mount up. Slocum ambled toward them. Was Rafferty getting ready to chase the errant sheriff?

Someone cried out as Slocum came closer. "Look, it's him."

Rafferty put his hands on his hips. "Son of a bitch. It *is* him. Now I guess we don't have to chase him."

Slocum grinned, tipping his hat in mockery. "Evenin', duster boys. Y'all out for a late ride?"

Rafferty turned toward the windows of the second floor. "Mayor, we found him. He's back."

Dunwood appeared at the dimly lighted opening. "Hanson, where in the hell have you been? You were supposed to check in with me an hour ago. I was just sending Rafferty to find you."

"Just lost track of time, Mayor," Slocum drawled. "I was so busy protectin' Rock Springs from outlaws."

Dunwood snarled and slammed the window shut. Slocum tipped his hat again and loped off toward the stable. He didn't even look back at the slack-faced posse of hired guns. He was almost glad he had returned. They probably would have caught him if he had ridden on.

The liveryman was glad to see him. Slocum stabled the gray and walked back to the hotel. He heard the door to the room opening while he was still on the stairs.

The woman was waiting for him, full of questions. "Where did you go? How could you leave me like that? They were looking for you. Do you know they were going to come after—"

Slocum lifted his finger to his lips. "Shh!"

"What?"

Slocum looked to the right and left and then whispered in her ear, "You were right, Addie. We can do it."

"Do what?" she asked impatiently.

"I want you to help me steal the gold."

Addie started to squeal. "I knew you'd see it my way. Oh, we're going to be rich, rich, rich!"

Slocum put his hand over her mouth. "Shut up. I don't want you to flap your lips all over town. If this gets back to Dunwood, he might decide to kill us before we can make a move."

Her eyes were wide. Slocum asked if she would hush up if he removed his hand. Addie nodded.

When he let go of her, she wrapped herself around him, kissing his face. She wanted it again. The lure of the gold had excited her.

Slocum pushed her away gently. "Not now. We got to plan. And I got to spend some more time on the roof, watching the offices."

Addie started to undress. "I can't help it. I'm as wet as a frog in a thunderstorm. Do it to me."

Slocum sighed. "I ain't in the mood."

Addie dropped to her knees. "Let's see if we can get you there. I know a few French tricks."

She unbuttoned him and took out his cock. Her lips slid up and down the flaccid length until he sprang to life. Now he wanted to do it. She had primed him well.

"You damned whore," he muttered.

She licked her lips. "Yes, and you better treat me like one."

Her ass hit the mattress. She spread her legs, inviting him in. Slocum decided to let everything else wait a while. He wanted to screw his wife.

18

Over the next three days, "Sheriff Hanson" and his "wife" established a routine in their hotel life. Every day Slocum awoke next to the woman, rubbing against her until they fell together. Then they got up, had a big breakfast downstairs, and lingered over a pot of coffee.

After breakfast, Slocum walked up and down the street on both sides, not speaking to anyone but making his presence known. Many of the citizens nodded to him and said friendly things, though they never stopped long enough to look him directly in the face.

His morning tour finished, Slocum usually went to the roof of the hotel for a couple of hours, watching the storefront at the Dunwood company. The hauling wagons were in and out, delivering, picking up, and leaving empty. A lot of travelers, miners, hunters, and grubstakers used Rock Springs as a stopoff in the crossing of the Divide. Coming and going, there seemed to be more transients than natives.

No wonder Dunwood didn't want the railroad to come. He had a lock on everything. The railroad would sure as hell change that. The trains always changed everything.

At midday, Slocum came down for lunch and a nap. Of course, Addie was there, smelling great. She had also purchased a new dress and some leather shoes. They'd end up napping together and wake up to more.

Slocum couldn't believe how much she wanted it. And how she could make him want it. No wonder the real Hanson had married her. She hadn't even blinked when her precious Brick went belly-up.

Nighttime saw dinner and another trip to the roof. Slocum marked the movements of everyone who came and went. He even charted the times with knife notches on the parapet. The move had to be quick, flawless. There had to be a weakness in the schedule somewhere, even if he hadn't found it yet.

Around ten, Slocum got his horse and made a slow circle around the town. He marched up and down the main street. It was really sort of stupid to be so visible, but no one had come after him. Things had calmed down considerably since he had blasted the Bateman brothers.

The tall man was trying to figure out a way to get the gold. There was a possibility that it had already been moved out in a loaded wagon. But Slocum had a hunch that Dunwood was keeping it nearby in his office. The only problem with getting in there was Dunwood himself. He never seemed to leave the place. He even slept at work. Didn't he have a home?

At the end of the third night, Slocum descended to talk with the woman. He told her it might be better if she tried to work her way inside, feel out Dunwood, get a line on the gold. Addie agreed, but she thought the best way to get to Dunwood was through Rafferty.

Slocum accused her of wanting to lie with Rafferty. She denied it. She even told the tall man they could really be man and wife if he wanted to tie the knot. Slocum replied that he didn't care how she got inside, just do it and find the gold.

They fought like man and wife, only this time they didn't fall into bed. Slocum buckled his gunbelt and headed out to ride his rounds. He got the gray from the stable and started walking the dark edges of the town line.

"Slocum!"

He stopped behind the saloon. Had the wind played a trick on his ears? He thought he had heard someone call his name.

"Slocum, over here."

A sulphur match glowed to life a few yards away. Slocum followed the light until it went out. He heard other riders circling him. Gable eased forward on a white mare.

"What do you want?" Slocum asked.

"Progress," Gable replied. "Have you had any?"

Slocum exhaled, shifting in the saddle. "I'm sendin' the woman inside. If she can get in."

"Excellent. Then what?"

Slocum shrugged. "I grab the gold and bring it to you."

"Fine."

"Anybody gonna cover my back?" Slocum asked.

Gable hesitated. "I—I'm not sure."

Slocum pointed a finger at him. "You ain't hangin' me out like a piece of cougar bait, railroad boy."

"If you can't do it," Gable said coldly, "then get ready to swing from a rope. Hyah!"

Gable turned the mare, disappearing into the night. The other riders followed him through the shadows. Slocum cut through the alley, emerging on the main street. He stabled the gray and returned to the hotel.

"What's wrong?" Addie asked.

"Nothin'. You start tomorrow."

She raised an eyebrow. "On Rafferty or Dunwood?"

"Whatever it takes, honey."

He'd keep looking for a way to get out of it, but until then, he had to stay after the gold. Slocum hadn't given up the idea of taking the strongbox for himself. It was like poker.

Play your cards close to your chest.

Watch the man across the table.

Never let anyone know what you got until the final bet is played.

Then pray like hell you get a winning hand.

"Damn," Slocum muttered. "Nothin'."

For five days, it had been the same. Addie had taken dinner to Dunwood in his office, fussing over him like a wife. But Dunwood didn't seem to take much interest. He loved his money and had time for little else.

As she had done four times before, Addie descended the stairs, coming out onto the street. This time was different than the others though—she had Rafferty with her.

"Son of a bitch."

He couldn't figure out why it bothered him so much to see her with the duster man. Maybe he was starting to care about her. She had done him right so far, sticking by him.

But a woman like Addie could switch loyalties pretty quick. He watched her as she warmed up to Rafferty. She giggled and teased, playing the virgin schoolgirl on a Sunday walk.

Slocum turned away from the sight. He went back to their room, waiting for her. Addie burst through the door in a jubilant mood.

"Seein' your boyfriend," Slocum scoffed.

"Oh, hush your mouth. It's gonna happen, honey. The big break has come. We're gonna be able to get all that gold."

Slocum squinted at her. "Says who?"

"Dunwood is leaving tomorrow morning," she replied. "The office is going to be empty."

"That *is* a break."

She sat next to him on the bed, touching his arm. "I sweet-talked old Rafferty there. He asked why couldn't I serve him dinner. I said, 'Where?' Then he said that Dunwood was leaving."

Slocum stood up. "I wonder how many of his men he's takin' with him?"

"Most of them," she replied. "Rafferty says he's the only one stayin' behind. Says we can go up to the office if we want."

"That bastard!"

Addie smiled and came off the bed, putting her hand on his shoulder. "I think it's sweet that you're so jealous."

"I ain't."

"Sure you are."

She kissed him lightly on the cheek.

Slocum drew back. "Not now."

"Where are you goin'?"

"On my rounds," he replied. "I *am* the sheriff. Or have you forgot?"

"Smartass."

"Whore!"

"Get out!"

He slammed the door. Something shattered behind him. He stomped down the hall to the stairs, ascending to the roof. He watched the Dunwood offices until he heard the footsteps behind him.

Addie had come to make amends. He had cooled off a little himself. They made up and did it right there on the roof. Addie got chilly so she went back, leaving him alone under the stars.

Slocum lay there for a long time, looking at the sky. As a boy, he had believed in heaven. After the war, he had believed in hell. Now here he was in a rough territory, plotting with Yankee scum to uphold the law. He tried to think about something else, like thousands of dollars in gold.

Why couldn't he escape with the strongbox?

He had done worse in his time.

Who would miss the gold? The railroad? They had a lot more money than Slocum. Mexico beckoned with its cheap women and even cheaper whiskey.

Across the street, the lights in the office were still burning. Slocum sat up, trying to catch a glimpse of Dunwood. He saw only shadows. What if the mayor really wasn't leaving at all?

Lying back again, he thought of attempting another run away from Rock Springs. Hell, Gable and Dunwood had men all over. He was likely to be chased by two posses, especially if he had the strongbox.

Slocum closed his eyes. He had strange dreams, waking to a cold dawn. He heard noises from the street below him.

A Concord coach was parked in front of Dunwood's offices. The stage had a fresh team and a driver. Some of Dunwood's other men sat on top of the vehicle. They carried rifles and shotguns.

"He's goin'."

Slocum watched until Dunwood came out of the building and boarded the coach. The stage rolled out of town, disappearing to the east. Where the hell was Dunwood going and how long before he came back?

Slocum started for the stairs. He had to wake the woman. It was time for them to go to work.

19

"How do I look, honey?"

Slocum gazed across the dim room, watching the woman as she primped in front of the mirror. The afternoon was almost gone, leaving them in the first shadows of evening. Addie had lit an oil lamp. Her new red dress made rustling noises when she moved. Slocum thought she looked damned good, but he wasn't about to tell her.

"Just get ready to do your job," he told her.

Addie made a mocking face and pursed her lips at him. "Ooh, I think my hubby's jealous."

She was right. Something inside Slocum hated the fact that she was going to spark another man. Especially Rafferty. But it had to be done.

"I'm gonna tell him that you're asleep," Addie said. "I don't want him to be worried that you might bust in on us."

Slocum nodded. He didn't care what she told him as long as they got the gold. He just hoped that Dunwood hadn't taken the strongbox with him when he left town.

She turned to him, posing. "How do I look?"

Slocum shook his head. "Don't bother me with that."

She pouted, putting her hands on her hips, thrusting forward her half-revealed bosom. "If you don't tell me how I look, I'm not gonna leave this room. I mean it!"

He exhaled and gave her a glance. "Addie, if you was Delilah, it wouldn't take much to get Samson to the barber."

She thought about it for a moment and then smiled. "Oh. Thanks, honey. I'll do you right when I get home tonight."

Slocum bolted out of the chair and grabbed her wrists. "This is serious, woman. There ain't gonna be no tonight. We're gonna grab the gold and stash it. Then we wait a few days before we vamoose."

"Let go, you're hurting me."

Slocum released his grip. "Sorry. Look, that stuff about stashin' the gold. That's bullshit."

She frowned. "What?"

"I might as well tell you the truth. The railroad boy, Gable, he wants the gold back. He said he'd turn us in to Dunwood if we didn't cooperate."

"Turn us in?" she whined. "For what?"

"He knows we ain't man and wife," Slocum replied. "He knows who I really am, that I ain't your precious Brick."

Addie grimaced, putting her hand to her forehead. "Okay, that's not fatal. We can just steal the gold and run."

"We won't get far. Gable has men all over," Slocum told her.

She patted his cheek with the flat of her hand. "Let's get the treasure first. Then we'll decide what to do."

"You got somethin' on your mind?"

"Trust me, honey."

How could he possibly trust anyone at this point? Slocum wondered.

Addie finished putting on her face and started for the door. She stopped to look back at him one more time. They didn't say anything. Addie left quickly, tapping down the stairs.

Slocum returned to the roof, watching as she went across the street with the food tray in her hand. Rafferty came out to meet her. They talked, laughed, and then headed up the stairs of Dunwood's building.

"Here it goes," Slocum muttered.

The lights did not burn in the outer office. They had gone to the back. Slocum knew where to situate himself so he could listen to them.

Stealing down from the roof, he went through the lobby to the street. He had to get to the rear alley. No one paid any attention to him as he slipped quietly between the buildings. He climbed the crates again to eavesdrop on Rafferty and the woman. They were starting to eat dinner.

"Good chicken," Rafferty said.

"Oh, they made it at the hotel," Addie replied. "I just came along to add the loving touch."

"What about your husband?"

"He's asleep. He'll snooze straight through till morning. I get bored at night. I need company."

"I thought you and Mr. Dunwood were gettin' friendly."

She laughed. "The Mayor. My no, he's old enough to be my pappy. I'm just grateful to him because he gave that worthless husband of mine a job."

Slocum flinched at his beloved's slight. He knew it was part of the act, but it still stung him. Did he really care about her? No, he just didn't want to share her with another man.

"More chicken?" she asked.

"Sure."

"No, Brick is all right," Addie went on, "but I wish he was more like, well, like you and the mayor. You know, sophisticated."

Slocum rolled his eyes. She was really heaping it on. The shit was getting too deep.

But Rafferty lapped it up. "Oh, yeah. How you mean?"

"You know, a man of means."

"Yeah." He laughed. "Hey, I do all right."

Addie sighed, shifting her tone of voice to a skeptical lilt. "Yes, I suppose, but you aren't really as wealthy as the mayor. I mean, aren't you just a gun for hire?"

Slocum heard the sound of silverware clinking as Rafferty dropped his fork onto the plate. "I ain't just a hired gun," he said defensively. "Mr. Dunwood is going to let me in for a cut."

She scoffed at him. "A cut of what? Nothing? When that railroad business gets here, he'll go belly-up."

"I don't care about that," Rafferty replied. "We got somethin' else to split between us."

"Like what?"

He hesitated. "Uh, I can't say."

Addie played him like a mouth harp. "Well, I best be going. I wouldn't want to have people get the wrong idea about me being up here, seeing as how I'm the sheriff's wife and all."

"No, don't go."

Addie giggled sweetly. "Why, Mr. Rafferty, I do think you are trying to get familiar with me."

"Stay."

"I mustn't—"

"Stay," he pleaded. "And I'll show you somethin'."

"I bet you will."

"No," Rafferty replied. "Somethin' good. Somethin' that me and the mayor are goin' to split fifty-fifty."

"Umm, I like the sound of that."

"Here—"

There were scuffling sounds in the office. Slocum listened to something heavy as it was dragged across the floor. Clinking of locks, squeaking of hinges. He had to be showing her the strongbox full of double eagles.

Addie gushed over the sight. "My word, where did you get all of this? It's so shiny. There must be a fortune here."

"Ten thousand five hundred," Rafferty replied.

"Oh, it's beautiful."

Suddenly everything grew quiet. Slocum knew what was happening. He wanted to jump through the window right then, but he figured it was better to wait awhile, let everything get going. Rafferty wouldn't be expecting the tall man from Georgia, not with his pants down.

"Oh, yes," Addie moaned in a low voice. "Let's get on the couch."

"You bitch," Rafferty said. "I knew you'd come around sooner or later. I knew you wanted it."

Slocum bit his lip.

Rafferty was trying to take control. "Pull out my Johnson. Do it, woman. Do it now."

Slocum reached for his sidearm. He had every intention of shooting Rafferty. He wasn't going to wait any longer. Throwing a leg up, he went through the casement.

Addie and the duster man were already on the couch. Rafferty was on top of her. He had it in her, pumping away.

Slocum tiptoed behind him and lifted the butt of the Peacemaker. Rafferty groaned just before the tall man brought the Colt down on the back of his head. Rafferty shivered, releasing inside her.

Addie cried out. She had also reached the moment of climax. Slocum rolled Rafferty off her and pulled her to her feet.

"You have your fun?" he asked.

Addie had sweated through the red dress. "You took your time gettin' here."

"Blame *me*."

They both looked down at Rafferty who lay unconscious on the floor. He was out for a while. Their eyes wandered over to the chest of gold.

"Look at it," Addie said.

Slocum was also captured by the lure of the yellow paydirt. Ten thousand, Rafferty had said. He could live forever in Mexico on that kind of money.

Addie grabbed his arm. "We've got to try."

He shook his head. "We can't."

"This is how we'll do it," Addie said. "We'll get one of Dunwood's wagons. Load up everything and hire a driver. Anybody, as long as it's not one of us. Then we can hide under a sheet of canvas while the driver takes us out of town. Gable will think it's just another one of Dunwood's wagons."

Slocum was half-listening. He made her say it again. Somehow, the woman's scheme seemed like it would work. It would be their only shot at the gold.

"We can do it," she insisted.

"Who will we get to drive us?"

"I don't know. Think."

Slocum had a sudden burst of inspiration. "The liveryman. He'll do it for me. We can tell him that Dunwood needs a load taken to Thayer."

"I know we can do it," she said lovingly.

Slocum's heart had begun to throb. What if they could pull it off? He could split with the woman down the trail and head south.

His eyes fell on Rafferty again. "We have to tie him up."

"I'll rip my petticoat," Addie volunteered.

"Damn!"

She frowned at him. "What?"

"We're gonna need saddlebags to put all this gold in."

"Why didn't you think of that before?" she challenged.

"Cause I didn't."

On the floor, Rafferty moaned. Slocum tapped him to send him back into darkness. He focused on the strongbox again. The gold had cast a spell over him.

"Are you going to get the saddlebags?" Addie asked.

Slocum nodded. "I reckon. I can ask the stableman if he wants to drive us. I'll offer him money."

"Gold, he'll take gold."

Slocum started toward the window. He wanted to go the back way so no one would see him. Emerging from the alley into the street, he looked in both directions, searching for more of Rafferty's men.

The town was deserted in the oncoming hues of night. Slocum hurried to the livery. He laid it out for the stableman who bought the story about Dunwood ordering an emergency run. The smithy would gladly drive the wagon.

Slocum asked for eight saddlebags, which the liveryman gladly gave him. He didn't even ask Slocum why he needed that many leather satchels. And the tall man from Georgia didn't offer any more information.

"I'll be ready to drive, Sheriff."

Slocum didn't even notice the invocation of his title. He went back into the street with the saddlebags thrown over his shoulder, reaching the alley without a single roving eye to mark his presence.

Addie was glad to see him. She still hadn't tied up Rafferty, though she had torn strips from her petticoat.

They filled the saddlebags and stacked them in a row. Slocum wiped the sweat from his brow. Thievery was getting to be hard work.

"I need some things from the room," Addie said.

Slocum squinted at her. "Now?"

"I'll get the bottle and the rest of my clothes."

He nodded slowly. "Okay. Meet me at the livery in a half hour."

She kissed him on the cheek. "I won't be late."

When she was gone, Slocum had the gold to himself. If he could haul it to the livery and get it loaded before Addie arrived, he could steal it all and never look back. Why not? He had as much right to the money as anyone else.

Slocum began to drag the bags toward the door. There was a wagon downstairs, parked on the street. It wouldn't take much to get it hitched and ready to roll. He had to tote all the bags to the street first.

He was hoisting two of the saddlebags when he heard the clicking of a pistol cylinder.

"That's far enough, rebel."

The boy called Hud Jones slid out of the shadows. In his frenzy with the gold, Slocum hadn't heard him coming. Jones held a Peacemaker in his hand. And the bore was aimed right at Slocum's head.

20

Slocum dropped the saddlebags and slowly straightened his body. "You got it all wrong, Jones."

The kid laughed. "You ain't stealin' the mayor's gold?"

"No," Slocum replied. "It was Rafferty. I caught him and stopped him."

"Sure," Jones replied, "but I don't care. See, Mr. Dunwood trusted me to stay and watch the fox. I'm guardin' the henhouse."

Slocum's hand eased down toward the butt of the Peacemaker. "Listen to me, Jones. We can both come out of this smellin' rosy."

"I will, rebel. Now, drop that hog leg on the floor and slide it toward me. Go on."

Slocum started to grab the pistol with his gun hand.

"Other paw," the kid told him.

Slocum reached across his chest and removed the Peacemaker from the holster.

"On the floor, rebel."

Slocum dropped the weapon.

"Now kick it to me."

The Colt slid across the wooden floor. Jones bent to pick it up, never taking his eyes off Slocum. The kid was sharp. Slocum tried to think of a trick to pull on him.

"Dunwood figured you'd try somethin'," Jones said. "That's why he left me back here. He gave me orders on what to do."

136

Slocum kept his eyes on the gun. "Look here, Jones. Let's divvy up this gold. You can take half."

"What about the woman?"

Slocum grimaced. "Forget about her. I got a wagon ready to roll. Hell, if you drove it out, who'd stop you?"

Slocum was hoping the kid would jump at the gold, but Jones never wavered. "Not me, rebel. I ain't havin' them other boys chase me down like a dog. Dunwood ain't gonna let nobody escape with this loot."

Before Slocum could say another word, Rafferty began to moan on the floor. He stirred slowly to life. The twin knots on his head had rendered him groggy. He took a few moments to realize what had happened.

"Damn. That rebel coldcocked me."

Jones waved the barrel of his Peacemaker. "Help him to his feet."

Slocum started to bend down. He figured he could go for the side arm inside Rafferty's duster. But Rafferty grunted and slapped him away.

"Get off me, Hanson," Rafferty bellowed. "I don't need you to help me up. I can stand."

Rafferty scuffled to his feet, reeling for a few seconds. He steadied himself against the desk. His eyes eventually focused on the empty strongbox.

"Damn, you was gonna steal it all, Hanson."

Jones nodded. "He sure was. But I stopped him."

Rafferty held out his hand toward the kid. "You did good, Hud. Now give me that gun."

Jones hesitated, staring at his boss. "I'm afraid I can't do that, Mr. Rafferty."

"What?"

"I can't do it," the kid repeated.

"Why not?"

"Because of this, Mr. Rafferty."

Jones thumbed the hammer and squeezed off the trigger. The gunshot was deafening in the tight space. Rafferty flew back against the wall, blood gushing from the hole in his chest.

Rafferty stayed on his feet for a few seconds. His eyes burned at the kid. He opened his mouth to say something, but the words never came. Rafferty fell forward on his chest, dying in a pool of crimson.

Slocum started to take a step toward the kid. Jones aimed the Colt at him. Slocum stopped dead.

"I ain't gonna shoot you unless you make me," Jones said.

Slocum glared at him. "Why?"

Jones shrugged. "Rafferty was a gob of spit. We all hated him. Even Dunwood can't stand him."

"You didn't have to kill him."

"Sure I did," Jones replied. "But I'm gonna say you shot him. Hell, you two was always goin' at each other anyways. We thought it was funny when you whipped his ass. I almost hate to do what I have to do."

"What's that?"

The kid exhaled. "Gonna have to put you in jail for the murder of Rafferty, Sheriff Hanson."

"You don't have to do that, kid," Slocum replied. "Just let me go. I'll get out of here and never look back."

"Somebody's got to take the fall. Might as well be you."

"Don't be a peckerwood, kid."

Jones waved the pistol at Slocum. "Dead or alive. What's it gonna be?"

Slocum wanted to stay alive. He thought he could reason with Dunwood. Hadn't he been cooperative all along?

"Come on, Sheriff," the kid said. "It's about time we remind you what the Rock Springs jail looks like."

Slocum flinched when he felt something biting his arm. He scratched the flea until it ran down to his wrist. Grabbing the nasty little critter, Slocum twisted it between his thumb and finger until it was dead.

"Lousy jailhouse."

The jail was the hole in the wall behind Dunwood's general store where Slocum had spent his first night in Rock Springs. Jones had left Slocum in the smaller cell, a six-by-six cage that looked like something from a circus. Jones told him that they sometimes used the cages for grizzlies or Indians.

Leaning back against the iron bars, Slocum did not curse his fate. He had brought it all on himself. The gold had made him crazy for a while. Now it really didn't matter that he had come to his senses. Unless he could reason with Dunwood, a hope that quickly faded.

The next morning, the mayor returned to Rock Springs, visiting Slocum in the cage. Dunwood had Jones and another man with him. Slocum asked if he could speak to the mayor alone. Dunwood obliged him.

"Sorry quarters," the mayor said. "You've fallen low, my friend."

Slocum tried the truth on the mayor. But Dunwood didn't want to hear it. He no longer needed Slocum to act as sheriff.

"I done everythin' you asked," Slocum said.

Dunwood sighed and shook his head. "It doesn't matter now, Hanson. If that is your name. No, there has been a fortuitous shift that will benefit all involved, except for you, my friend."

"Me?" Slocum asked.

Dunwood stayed back, staring through the bars. "Yes, you see, I've made my peace with the rail company. I'm going to be the station manager when the train finally comes in."

Slocum glared back at him. "What's that got to do with me?"

Dunwood shrugged. "Simple. You are now expendable. And I need someone to take the fall for killing Rafferty."

"But Jones killed him!"

"Of that, I have no doubt. Hud wanted to replace Rafferty, which he has, at least until someone kills him."

"So set me free," Slocum replied.

"It's not that simple. You see, I want to keep the gold and the only way to do that is to have someone else steal it. And that someone is you."

Slocum grabbed the bars, pressing his face into the cold iron. "I didn't steal anythin', Dunwood."

The mayor gestured to the air. "Ah yes, but who else knows that? By the time I tell the story, you will have made off into the mountains, hiding the gold where no one will ever find it. You'll take the secret to the gallows with you. They'll flock to your hanging like sinners to the fires of hell."

"You ain't got to do this, Dunwood. You hear me? Just let me go. You can say Rafferty hid the gold in the hills."

Dunwood smiled slightly. "No, the people need to see a neck stretched at the end of a rope. And who better to swing than a double-dealing sheriff? Good day, Hanson."

"My name ain't Hanson."

"I don't care," Dunwood replied. "That's what they'll be callin' you when they lower the noose over your head."

Dunwood left in a hurry. Slocum wondered how long it would take him to get things stirred up. The rest of the morning was quiet, but by noontime, Slocum could hear the hammers and saws from the street. He knew what they were building— a gallows to hang the new sheriff.

21

By dusk, the hammering had stopped and Slocum had grown tired of scratching his fleabites. He had been so close to escaping. Now he was going to be served up to the citizens of western Wyoming, a hanging platter to sate their appetite for blood. In his heart, he tried to blame Gable for making him stay, but he could not carry on the deception. He had stayed out of greed, to try for the strongbox one more time. He had no one to blame but himself.

Gable. Where was the railroad man now that Slocum had been locked up in the animal cage they called a jail? Did he really believe that Slocum had hidden the gold in the mountains, never to be found again?

"My own damn fault," he muttered to himself.

He never should have fallen in with money people. Men like Dunwood and Gable cared about only one thing—their riches. Everybody else could go hang when gold was on the line. A poor fellow didn't have a chance if he got caught in the web.

Slocum shifted around, trying to get comfortable. His whole body ached from the confinement in the cell. He could not stand up. He had to lean back with his head on cold steel.

"Damn me," he whispered. "Damn me to hell."

There didn't seem to be any way of escaping. Even if he did manage to get out of the cell, Dunwood's men were probably stationed all over town. The mayor wasn't about to let his scapegoat out of the pen.

Closing his eyes, he drifted off into an uneasy slumber, dreaming of the woman. Addie's voice filled his head. He heard her screeching at the top of her lungs. The words were so clear that he startled awake.

But the voice did not stop. Addie kept on screaming. She was outside his cell, arguing with one of the guards.

"I'm going in to see him!" she cried. "And you won't stop me. Get out of my way this instant."

Slocum smiled a little. He figured she was a lot better than most of the women he had known in his life. She had a certain tenacity about her, a will that would not let her give up.

"I don't care what the mayor said," she railed. "You're gonna let me in there or I'm gonna—what? Oh yes, go ahead and search me. Put your filthy hands all over me. That's what you want to do anyway."

Silence in the shadows. Slocum imagined that the guard would take advantage of her. Would she really try to bring him a weapon? Maybe he would have a chance if the woman was still on his side.

Outside, Addie was in fine form. "Is that enough? Or do you want to play with my titties some more? Then open this goddamn door before I—"

The key rattled in the lock. Addie stepped through the dingy doorway with a tray in her hands. She stood there for a moment, waiting for her eyes to adjust to the dim light.

"Hello, Addie."

She moaned when she saw him crouched in the cage. "Oh, you poor thing. What have they done to you?"

Slocum sighed. "I been et by a wolf and shit off a cliff."

Addie came to the cell, kneeling down in front of him. "I brought you some food. Stew and bread. Are you hungry?"

"My last meal, huh?"

"No, not really."

Slocum squinted at her through the bars. "What do you mean by that?"

It was Addie's turn to sigh. "Rumor is that Dunwood is gonna wait a few days to draw in the suckers."

"Figures. Let me have that grub."

She tried to push the tray through the bars, but there wasn't enough room. Slocum had to settle for being fed with a spoon. He was ashamed to eat like a hog in a pen, but he had no choice. As bleak as his chances were, he still had to maintain his strength, in case he got an opportunity to bolt.

When he had finished, he drew back, gazing at the woman's pretty face. "What else have you heard?"

She shook her head. "Not much more. Just that Dunwood got right with the railroad. He says you took the money though, that you hid it somewhere in the mountains. That's gonna draw as many people as your—"

"Go ahead and say it," he scoffed. "As many people as my hangin'!"

"I'm so sorry, honey."

"John."

"What?"

"My name's John," he replied. "John Slocum. I wanted you to know my real name before they lynched me."

She smiled. "John. I like that. Oh, I can't tell you how much I miss you in that bed. I mean, I feel bad that I'm walkin' away from this scot-free. I woulda been with you if I hadn't gone back to the hotel."

Slocum didn't tell her that he had planned to leave her, to take the gold with him. He needed her. She might be his last hope and he didn't want her mad at him. Women could get mad over little things like abandonment.

"I miss you too," he said softly.

"Oh, John, is there any way out? I mean, I didn't care that much for Brick, but I—well, I think I'm in love with you."

He leaned forward a little. "Then do somethin'."

"Like what?"

"I don't know. Hell, you're two times better at schemin' than I am. You can figure somethin'."

"I—I don't know, John. My hands are tied. I'd be lost if Dunwood cut off my hotel privileges."

Slocum snorted angrily. "He's gonna cut off a lot more'n that for me. You hear me? I'm finished."

She put her hands on the bars. "I'll try, John. I swear. But if I can get you out of this, you have to promise to take me with you. Do you hear? I don't want to be left alone."

"I will."

"Promise!"

He took a deep breath. "All right, I promise."

"Swear on the honor of Dixie!"

"Addie!"

"I mean it!"

He nodded. "Okay."

"Say it."

"I swear on the honor of Dixie," he muttered.

She smiled broadly. "Oh, John, I just know everything is gonna be all right. Now, kiss me."

Reluctantly, Slocum leaned forward. Their lips touched between the iron bars. Addie's tongue twisted in his mouth.

She broke away suddenly. "I miss you so much. Here, look at my titties. I want you to touch them."

Freeing her breasts, she pressed them against the bars so Slocum could fondle her. He found himself with a perilous thought—what if this was his last chance to see a woman naked? He tried to kiss her nipples but it was too awkward with the bars in the way.

"Lemme feel your pussy," he said.

Without a word, Addie hiked up her dress, hunching against the cage with her pelvis. Slocum grabbed for the moist, furry opening, working his fingers inside. When he tried to pull his hand away, Addie grabbed his wrist and held him there.

"More," she said. "Feel me, honey. Feel me deep."

He kept on with his manipulations, but the posture was not very satisfying for either one of them. Addie begged him to take out his cock. They did everything they could, but penetration was impossible through the cell.

"Here, let me hold it," she whispered.

Slocum leaned back, thrusting his hips upward. Addie reached through the bars, grabbing his cock. She worked him by hand until he released. Addie then broke down and started to cry.

"I'm so sorry," she sobbed. "I didn't want it to turn out like this. I really care about you, John. I really do."

"Then get me out of here," Slocum challenged.

"I'll try, honey. I swear I will. Kiss me again."

Their lips met through the bars but this time there was no rush of passion. The iron felt cold on their cheeks, as cold as the skin of a dead man. Addie drew back, buttoning the front of her dress, straightening the folds of the fabric. Picking up the tray, she started for the door.

"Thanks," Slocum said.

Addie looked over her shoulder. "I won't let 'em hang you, John. I swear on my husband's grave."

"Just see that you don't have to bury your husband twice," he replied.

"Good-bye, John."

When she left, the key rattled in the door lock that separated the cage from the outside world. Somehow, Slocum felt better about his chances. But when he awoke the next morning to the sound of hammers and saws at work again on the gallows, the good feeling retreated in a hurry.

22

After four days, Slocum had to wonder if the fires of hell were going to be any worse than incarceration in the flea-infested cage. The tall man from Georgia figured he would end up on the other side of paradise, burning with old Pitch. It was too late to try to square things away with St. Peter. Maybe the Devil would be better company than the swarming vermin.

They left Slocum alone except for the one meal a day that was brought in by Hud Jones. Slocum didn't speak a word to the kid, he didn't even look at him. Jones didn't say anything to him either. What was there to say? The cards had been rolled and Slocum was staring at a low-pair loser.

Slocum had to eat by grabbing handfuls and pulling the food through the bars. He gobbled it down like an animal. His eyes were wide in the shadows, his body coiled in a hunching curve. If he could have gotten to Jones, Slocum would have ripped out his throat with his bare hands.

Why didn't they just go ahead and hang him? Surely Dunwood had drawn a crowd by now. By Slocum's calculations it was Friday, so anyone who was coming should have arrived.

"Son of a bitchin' bastard," Slocum muttered under his breath.

The tall man's heart filled with rage when he thought about his captors. He wasn't going to let them hang him if he could help it. As soon as he saw an opening, he'd make his move, grab a gun or another weapon, force them to kill him, even if he had to fight with his bare hands.

"Son of a bitchin' *Yankee* bastards."

Who would he try to kill? Dunwood or Gable if they were around. Or both. They had joined up to doom him, scavengers of a feather. He saw their throats seeping—and then pouring—blood.

How? Just move when they gave him room. They had to take him out of the cell eventually. He would walk upright like a man again before he met his Maker.

The door opened in front of him. Jones stepped in. He had come to get the dinner dishes. Slocum put the kid on the list of those to be killed in the mayhem of revenge.

"You're a pitiful sight, rebel," Jones said.

This will be *you* one day, Slocum thought. Men like Dunwood and Gable didn't care who got hurt as long as they made their money. They'd do something bad to Jones when it suited them.

Jones picked up the dishes from the floor. "Chowin' down like a mule. You sunk mighty sorry, rebel."

And you're just treading water, the tall man said to himself.

"Hangin's tomorrow," Jones said. "Saturday. The place is hoppin' with spectators. You ready, *Sheriff*?"

Slocum's green eyes lifted, burning through the shadows to glare at the kid. Jones had said the one word that could get to Slocum. Posing as a lawman had brought on the bad luck, the jinx, the hex. A man just couldn't go too far against his own nature and expect to win. Slocum had played the lawman, a mistake that now extracted a heinous price.

"I knew that'd get a rise out of you," Jones said. "Tell me, rebel. Why'd you do it? Was it the woman?"

"Shut up!"

Jones chortled. "Dunwood won't let her come to see you. Hell, she ain't been around all week. You think she's found herself another beau?"

Slocum closed his eyes, gritted his teeth, squeezed the bars until his knuckles turned white. He had to die with dignity. Nobody was going to turn him into a cowering, caged dog.

"Hang tight," the kid jabbed. "I'll be back."

Slocum tried to relax his body. He felt some strength there. His anger and hatred were fuel for the fire. What if he could only get to one of them? Who would he kill if he had to choose?

The lanky son of Dixie had no perception of how long Jones was gone before he came back. He just looked up and the kid was standing there. Two armed men flanked Dunwood's new right hand man.

"I'm gonna open the door," Jones said slowly. "When we step back, you crawl out on all fours."

Slocum's chance had arrived. The murderous desire coursed through his veins. He tasted vengeance in his dry mouth.

Jones rotated the key in the lock. The cell door clinked open. Jones drew back between the other two men.

"Come on out, Johnny Reb."

Slocum hesitated, trying to focus his eyes in the dimness. He was pretty sure the two guards had shotguns. The kid rested his hand on the butt of his Peacemaker.

"I said move, Cracker!" Jones yowled.

Slocum had to test his body. Slumping forward, he put down his hands, feeling the hard floor beneath him. His knees also touched the packed earth. When he started to crawl, he felt some pain and tightness, but nothing that would get in the way.

"Look at 'im," said one of the men. "He's like a damned dog."

"Yeah," Jones laughed. "Come on, doggy. Here pooch."

Slocum eased out of the cage, lifting his eyes to the figures before him. He had to spring quickly, leave the floor and grab one of the shotguns. In such tight quarters, the other shotgun man probably wouldn't get off a shot right away because he would have to swing the barrel.

"Stop right there," Jones said.

Slocum kept crawling. Grab the shotgun on the left, swing it around into the kid's chest. Boom! One gone. Maybe two if the angle was right.

The clinking of chains filled the damp air. They were going to manacle him like a slave. But where the hell were they taking him to now? The hanging was still a day away.

"Cuff him," Jones ordered.

Slocum saw the man lean his shotgun against the wall. He came from the right with the chains. Slocum decided to go then.

Screeching at the top of his lungs, he sprang from the floor, jumping toward the shotgun man on the left. Slocum's legs dug hard, but something cramped as soon as he tried to stretch out. The pain stopped him dead. He fell short with his fingers brushing the front of the shotgun man's duster.

The butt of a scatter-gun rose over Slocum's fallen body. "I'll teach you to try to—"

Jones stopped the gun butt from crushing Slocum's skull. "No."

"Why not? Did you see what he did?"

Jones pushed him back. "Forget it. Dunwood wants him in one piece. We've got to get him cleaned up for the hangin'."

"Yeah," the chain man replied. "You cain't hang a boy that's all beat up. It ain't as much fun."

The shotgunner started to move toward Slocum. "Let's drag his worthless ass over to the bathhouse—"

Some pain was easing in Slocum's calves. He thought he could move again. And the shotgun was coming right toward him.

Jones stopped the man and pushed him away again. "No. Be careful with this one. He took those boys we sent to rob the stage. Remember?"

"Aw, he ain't—"

"Put it in a barrel! Chain him."

The other man hesitated. "Well . . . cover me or somethin'."

Slocum gazed up at the kid. Jones drew his Peacemaker and bent down, putting the barrel on Slocum's neck. The iron felt cold and damp.

"One move and you're splattered, rebel," Jones said. "I don't care if Rock Springs is cheated out of a hangin'. You hear?"

Slocum grunted. The chain man went to work. He manacled Slocum's hands to another circle of chain around his waist and then clamped a short length to fix his ankles together. Slocum wasn't going to run away or throw a punch at anybody. They had him for now.

"Get him on his feet," Jones barked.

Slocum felt his legs again. They cramped but he managed to keep standing. Suddenly his stomach began to churn. His green eyes would not focus, his head spun with his first few steps.

The shotgun butt urged him toward the door. "Go on, you stupid bastard. You still got work to do."

Staggering forward, Slocum maintained his balance as he stumbled through the doorway. Jones gave him a little push, which caused the tall man to fall face-first into the alley.

"Shit, Jones, I thought we wasn't s'posed to hurt him."

Jones slammed the toe of his boot into Slocum's ribs. "This ain't gonna show. Here, rebel. Take this." He kicked him again.

The pain in Slocum's side sharpened and then spread into a slightly duller ache. They got him to his feet again, dragging him toward a bathhouse that was no doubt owned by Dunwood.

Inside the bathhouse, oil lamps burned all around a huge, steaming wooden tub. Jones tore the clothes from Slocum's body, stripping him down to nothing. Then the kid ordered the tall man to climb into the tub.

"No," the chain man said.

Jones scowled at him. "What?"

"They'll rust up. I paid good money for them chains. I don't want to get them wet."

Jones sighed. "Okay, take 'em off. But give me your shotgun first. And hold that other scatter-gun on him."

"Aw, he don't look that tough, Hud."

"Just do it!"

Four barrels stared darkly at Slocum while the man undid the chains. Slocum eased into the hot water. The heat took away some of the pain.

Jones tossed a bar of soap into the tub. "Scrub good. Go get the barber. Tell him we'll be ready soon. And get those new duds from the general store."

As the chain man was departing, Dunwood came in, squinting through the orange lamp glow. "How is he?"

Jones laughed. "He'll be ready to walk through that little trapdoor. You found a hangman yet?"

Dunwood glared at the kid. "That's no concern of yours. Just have him ready to go at noon tomorrow."

Dunwood stomped out in a huff. He was nervous. Had something gone wrong with the railroad? Slocum was grasping at anything that might give him an edge or a chance to strike.

"Scrub it, rebel."

Slocum rubbed up a lather between his hands. They were really trimming him out for the crowd. A bath, a shave, and new clothes. The barber was coming, they had said it. Slocum would probably get a haircut too.

"You're clean enough," the kid said after a while. "Stand up."

They held both scatter-guns on him. Jones threw Slocum a towel. He told the tall man to dry off.

"Hoo-wee," the shotgunner said. "Look at that Johnson on him. A dad-blamed home wrecker there."

"Aw, shut up," the kid bellowed.

They both laughed and for a moment they were looking at each other. Slocum started to step out of the tub. The shotguns reminded him to be still. He wrapped the towel around his waist and stood there helplessly.

They waited until the barber came. Slocum sat on a barrel while the man trimmed his hair. Then the barber took out a cup and a brush.

"What are you gonna do?" the kid asked.

"Dunwood wants me to shave him," the barber replied.

Jones waved the scatter-gun. "Go ahead, but be careful. He can be a mean one."

The barber lathered Slocum's face. A sharp blade scraped away the stubble. Slocum held steady, keeping his eyes on his captors. They were starting to relax. The scatter-guns rested on their hips.

The razor came down again. This time Slocum grabbed the barber's wrist, taking the blade away from him. He held the barber's head in the crook of his arm. The razor rested against the man's throat.

"Let me go or I kill him," Slocum challenged.

Jones was stunned for a moment, but then he laughed. "Go ahead and kill him, rebel. See if I care."

The barber squealed. "Noo, don't—"

Slocum did not flinch with the razor. "I mean it, Jones. Let me go or I open up his neck."

"Do it," the kid chortled. "What the hell do we care about one pussy-faced hair chopper? I mean, we still got the guns. And it'll make a good tall one to tell. The mad dog sheriff kills an innocent barber."

"No, please, don't let him kill me!"

Slocum saw that the bluff wasn't going to work. He let go of the barber and dropped the razor on the floor. He heard the chains clinking again.

"Smart move, rebel," Jones said.

The barber pointed a trembling finger at the kid. "I'm going to tell Mayor Dunwood about this."

"Go shave your ass!" the kid replied.

Slocum stared down at the scatter-guns again. He hadn't totally resigned himself to the inevitability of dying. But the moment of truth was sure as hell drawing close in a hurry.

23

Jones made Slocum dress up in the same kind of starchy clothes he had worn as sheriff. The stiff fabric irritated the fleabites on his arms and legs. He would have scratched, but they had tied his hands behind his hips again. The ankle bracelets also returned to hobble him. How the hell was he going to kill them if they kept him hog-tied?

"What about his boots, Hud?"

Jones shrugged. "Let him go barefoot. Ain't no need of wastin' a good pair of boots on this peckerwood."

The man frowned. "Aw, I was plannin' on takin' 'em off 'im when he was gone. I mean, we are about the same size."

Jones rolled his eyes. "Just shut up and get him over to the offices."

They took him down a dark back alley to the rear entrance of Dunwood's place. Slocum climbed the stairs to Dunwood's private office. The room was almost dark. A lone candle made a circle of radiance that seemed to deepen the shadows in the corners.

"Lay down over there," Jones said, pointing with the barrel of the shotgun. "Get some sleep."

Slocum waddled and clanked toward the cot that had been set up in the middle of the room. He hoped Jones would leave him with only one guard, but all three of them stayed, with their weapons. Slocum had no choice but to lie down on the cot.

153

"Don't know why he wants to sleep," one of them said. "He's gonna be sleepin' forever, tomorrow that is!"

Jones glared at him. "Shut up."

"Aw, Hud, I wasn't—"

"Shut up, I tell you!"

Why the hell was Jones getting so jumpy? Slocum wondered. Did he have a plan of his own? Maybe he had his eyes on the gold after all.

"What's wrong, Hud?"

"Nothin'," Jones replied. "I just don't want nobody jinxin' this. After things settle down, Dunwood is gonna give us a piece of the pie."

Slocum laughed. "You think so, huh?"

Jones scowled at him. "Shut up, rebel."

"Did Rafferty get his cut of the pie?" Slocum challenged.

"No, he got a cut of the dirt when they covered him over."

The kid thumbed back the twin hammers of the scatter-gun. "One more word, boy, and I cheat the hangman."

Slocum took a little bit of satisfaction in riling the nervous kid. Lying back on the cot, he kept his eyes open, waiting for the dawn. But the cot was too comfortable, at least compared to the cell. He drifted off in a peaceful slumber, waking to the sudden blaring of brass horns.

The light blinded him when he opened his green eyes. Music seemed to swell all around him. Was he already at the pearly gates of St. Peter? No, it was only the sunlight, something he had not seen in almost a week.

"Hop to, rebel," Jones said. "You got a big day ahead of you. Wouldn't want you to be late for your necktie party."

Slocum tried to sit up but the chains held him on the cot. Jones helped him get his body erect. His bare feet dangled over the edge of the cot, brushing the cold floor.

"Looks like it's gonna be a sunny day," Jones went on. "You ready?"

Slocum bristled, but he could not move more than a couple of inches toward Jones. He almost fell off the cot. Jones pushed him back with the barrel of the scatter-gun.

"Give it up, Johnny Reb."

Slocum spat at him. "Kiss my ass."

Jones just laughed. "Dunwood is gonna pay the hangman to tie the knot in back of your head, boy. Your neck ain't gonna snap. You're gonna strangle to death in a slow-like way. Kickin' and twitchin' at the end of that rope. It might take you a hour to die."

Jones would have gone on with his horrible speech, but someone knocked on the door to interrupt him.

"Yeah?"

"Breakfast for the Sheriff."

Slocum winced again at the sound of the word. "I ain't no sheriff!"

Jones opened the door and took the tray from one of his men. "What time is it?"

"Eleven-thirty," the man replied. "Mr. Dunwood says to let him eat and then get started. Figure to bring him out in fifteen minutes."

Jones nodded and shut the door.

A tray full of breakfast was placed in front of Slocum. It was a real country repast. Eggs; bacon, side meat, potatoes, grits, biscuits, and gravy poured on everything. Slocum's last meal. Maybe his last chance.

"I need a free hand," he said.

Jones sighed. "Unlock his left one." He lifted the scatter-gun, keeping it trained on the tall man.

When Slocum's hand was loose, he began to spoon the food to his mouth. It was hot and thick, though it could have used some black pepper to spice up the milk gravy. After he had finished, he looked at Jones's neck, wondering how much damage he could do with a spoon.

"Drop the silverware in the plate," Jones said. "And wipe your mouth. You eat like a pig."

"You wouldn't let me use my right hand," Slocum replied.

"Shut up and use that napkin."

Slocum lifted the cloth napkin to his face. As he wiped his lips, his nose caught the scent of something familiar. The napkin had been doused with Addie Hanson's strong perfume. Was it a good-bye message? Or did the former Kansas City chippy have a plan? Was she signaling him with the perfume? Or just telling him that she was sorry he had to die?

"Time to go," Jones said.

Slocum knocked the tray away from him. He struggled with his bonds, but there was no way to get free. He had always sworn to himself that he would never die by hanging. Now he was going to break that oath.

"Don't fight it," Jones said. "You can't get out of this, boy. You hear me? It's over for you."

Slocum stopped struggling. He lay still for a moment. Then Jones helped him to his feet.

Slocum reeled like a dying top, wobbling on his rubbery legs. The cage had made him too weak. And the anger had abandoned him. He felt numb. He could barely walk toward the door.

"He's gonna need help down those stairs, Hud."

"No," Jones said. "Let him walk it by hisself."

Vertigo set in the moment Slocum perceived the angle of the stairwell. He reached for the wall, but it wasn't there. His knees buckled and he tumbled over the steps, hurtling toward the bottom.

"Damn, Hud, get him before he—"

Jones took the steps two at a time. But Slocum wasn't in any shape to run. He could barely breathe. The bellows was pumping in his heart, churning the fire through his chest.

"Get up, you rebel bastard."

Jones reached down for him. Slocum grabbed his wrist. He managed to sink his front teeth into the back of the kid's hand. Jones screeched and knocked Slocum away. Slocum found himself grinning with satisfaction.

"You all right, Hud?"

Jones looked at his bleeding hand. "I can't wait to see him swing. Put him out in the street. Let the crowd have him."

When the door flew open, the horns struck up again. A small band of musicians played a rough version of "Dixie." Slocum staggered out the front door. He teetered in front of the mob. A bobbing sea of gawking faces parted before him, clearing a path.

"There he is," someone cried.

"Look, he's bleedin', there's a cut on his head."

"Hang 'im."

"Lynch the traitor sheriff."

Slocum gazed over their heads, seeing the gallows for the first time. The noose had been strung. The hangman had donned his hood.

"Outta the way! Stop gaping!" the kid cried.

Jones and his men surrounded Slocum. A shotgun butt prodded him down the aisle that formed as they passed through the crowd. They started toward the wooden structure that had been erected for Slocum's execution.

"You want a preacher?" Jones asked.

Slocum spat at him again. Jones slapped him. The crowd cheered, so the kid slapped him again.

The tall man took both blows with a smile. "What's wrong with your hand, kid? Huh? Who bit you?"

Jones snarled and gave up. He used his men to drive Slocum up the steps to the gallows platform. A sandbag sat on the trap door, which sprang open suddenly and dropped the bag to the ground.

Slocum turned slowly, gazing out over the mob. He was looking for Addie. Suddenly her face appeared in a window on the second story of the hotel. She was waving a red handkerchief.

He nodded at the woman. When she knew she had his attention, she nodded slowly, gazing wide-eyed in his direction. What was she trying to tell him?

"No," he muttered.

Addie had disappeared from the window. Slocum felt a hand on his shoulder. He turned to see the mayor of Rock Springs staring at him.

"I'm sorry it came to this," Dunwood said.

"No you ain't."

Dunwood wheeled toward the mob, waving a hand out over them. "Ladies and gentlemen, this is what comes of a double-crossing lawman in this territory."

The throng cheered his declaration. There must have been five hundred of them. Fathers were lifting their sons for a better look. Women averted their eyes but only enough so they could still see.

Slocum looked for Addie again, but she was nowhere to be seen.

"And furthermore," the mayor pontificated, "some people would vote to disband this fine territory of Wyoming, but we shall not have it so. If you elect me as your territorial governor, I'll see to it that you are protected, and that you get the most from the railroad—which will be here in no less than four months!"

Slocum looked sideways at the gray-haired man. He was politicking, stumping for votes on the tall man's grave. He worked them into a frenzy and then turned toward Slocum with a maniacal preacher's gleam in his eyes.

"What have you to say for yourself?" Dunwood asked.

Slocum's head rolled on his neck, marking the men with shotguns. Jones was looking at his injured hand. The other two had drawn down on Slocum. No escape. This was really it.

"Make peace with your Maker," somebody called from the crowd.

"Speech!"

"Repent, sinner!"

A dumb smile spread over Slocum's face. Somehow it seemed sort of funny. They were all gaping up at him from the street.

"Have you any last words for these good people?" Dunwood asked.

Slocum figured he had better give them a show. "Well, I ain't done nothin' wrong, Mayor."

"Boo!"

"Liar!"

"Repent, child of Lucifer!"

The tall man from Georgia shook his head. "There's a snake in this town, folks. His name is Dunwood. Watch out or he'll steal everythin' you got and then sell it back to you with interest."

"That's enough!" the mayor cried.

"Kiss my ass, Dunwood."

The mayor lunged toward Slocum. But the tall rebel was ready for him. Slocum couldn't move much, but he managed to lean into Dunwood. The gray-haired man bounced off him and fell into the crowd.

Stunned expressions covered the faces of the spectators as they fell silent. They couldn't believe what Slocum had done. Dunwood lay in the street with his neck broken. His body twitched as he died.

Slocum laughed bitterly. "Enough of that."

He started to hobble toward the edge of the gallows. He wanted to throw himself on top of Dunwood. But then the kid was there, pushing him back with the bore of the shotgun.

Slocum's bare feet hit the square of the trapdoor. He felt the wood give a little as it tightened.

Jones slid the noose òver Slocum's head. "Knot behind, worm bait. You're gonna die slow."

Slocum spat in his face.

Jones backed away and signaled the hangman.

Suddenly Slocum had lots of energy. His pain had left him in the last moments of his life. He looked down into the crowd for a second. Addie was right there, waving at him. Why was she smiling?

"Do it," Jones cried.

The hangman tripped the switch and the trapdoor opened, falling out from under Slocum. The rope tightened. He swung there with his feet dangling over the street.

24

The noose dug into Slocum's windpipe, cutting off the air. Panic set in, followed by a lightness in his head. Suddenly a light began to glow in front of him. It no longer mattered if he was alive or dead.

A shotgun blast erupted from the crowd. Balls of lead cut through the thick rope, snapping the cord and freeing Slocum to drop to the ground. He hit limply, rolling on his side.

The light did not go away. Slocum felt warm and weightless. He knew his eyes were open, but he could only see the eerie glow.

His body seemed to slide along the ground. Dust swirled up around him but Slocum perceived the dirt as clouds. He thought he was flying through the yellow sky of morning.

Gunshots and confusion surrounded the tall man from Georgia, but he did not hear anything. He was unaware of the riders who had surged through the crowd on black horses, firing pistols and rifles into the air. When Dunwood's henchmen opened fire on the intruders, the riders dismounted, found cover, and then shot back at them.

Slocum's chest burned, reminding him that he was still inside his body. He gasped for breath. It was hard sucking wind through his aching throat. He coughed and wheezed, taking short breaths.

Suddenly he did not want to die. He heard the gunshots. People were shouting, screeching, rushing by him. Their shapes were just blurred shadows, but he knew they were in a frenzy.

The light went dim above him. Slocum became aware that the sun was no longer on his face. Another shape appeared over him. At first he thought it was the Devil himself.

He had gone away from the light, into the dark. He was going to die anyway and Satan had sent his blackest demon to lead the way. Slocum didn't want to pass through into the netherworld.

"No!"

A tender hand stroked his forehead. "It's okay, honey. We saved you from that noose. You're gonna be fine."

Slocum knew the voice. It was the voice of an angel. Addie Hanson had plucked him from beneath the gallows. She had dragged him through the crowd to safety. It was the second time she had saved his life.

"Is he okay, Mrs. Hanson?"

Slocum heard the man's voice. He couldn't place it at first. Who the hell had been willing to help Addie?

"He's gonna live," Addie said. "Here, let me look at that throat."

"I better get these stable doors closed."

The liveryman! He had always liked Slocum. Addie had talked him into lending a hand.

The light grew even dimmer as the stable doors closed. Slocum felt the woman's fingers on his neck. It was still hard for him to breathe.

"You got a mean rope burn there, John," Addie said. "Here, this might hurt but it's got to be done."

She rubbed something oily on his skin. It didn't burn at all. In fact, the cool balm eased the pain of the rope.

The liveryman kneeled down next to him. "Here, let him eat a piece of bread. It might open up his throat."

Slocum shook his head. "Water," he said in a low rasp.

Addie reached beneath the folds of her dress. "I got somethin' even better. Here, take a shot."

Addie touched the neck of a small bottle to his lips. The whiskey warmed his throat and his chest. He felt a jolt through his body. Addie gave him another snort to double the effect.

Slocum focused on Addie's kind eyes. "What happened?"

She sighed. "Gable got word that you were going to hang. He figured you was caught tryin' to recover the gold for him.

He wasn't about to let Dunwood murder you."

"I'm one of Gable's men," the liveryman offered. "I been watchin' you all the time. I knew what Dunwood was tryin' to do."

"Agreement," Slocum whispered. "Dunwood. Railroad."

"Just a trick to buy time," Addie replied. "Gable was never going to throw in with Dunwood. He wanted him out of the way."

More shots echoed from the street. Slugs bounced off the thick planks of the livery. Someone ran to the door and banged wildly, begging for shelter. Slocum and the others just sat there, listening to the melee.

"They're gonna be at it for a while," Addie said. "Get me a dipper of water, smithy."

"Sure."

Addie mixed a white powder with the water. "Drink this, honey," she said to Slocum. "I got it from the man at the general store. It's an elixir. It'll make you feel better."

The liquid tasted bitter. Slocum choked on it and had to be given more clear water. For a moment, he felt sick to his stomach, but a few minutes later the powder took hold and he was floating again.

"What the hell was that?" he heard himself ask.

"Opium," Addie replied. "I think."

Slocum tried to lift his head. He was finally able to sit up in the pile of straw. Addie had nursed him back to life.

"More water," he said hoarsely.

A sweat broke as he guzzled from the dipper. The pain seemed to flow out of his body. He started to stand but the chains were still binding him.

"I can take care of those manacles," the liveryman offered. "I'll have you loose in no time."

He ran to get his tools.

Slocum looked into Addie's smiling face. "What are you up to, woman?"

"What makes you think I'm up to anything?"

"The look on your face," he replied. "You look like a blue jay who just caught a worm."

She leaned forward, kissing him on the mouth. Her lips did as much as the opium to revive him. She drew back, still grinning.

"You ain't answered me," he said.

She bent her mouth to his ear. "We're gonna steal the gold," she said. "All of it. Now."

Slocum tried to laugh but it came out as a cough. Outside, the guns were raging on, fighting the battle of Rock Springs. How were they going to get through all that chaos to find the gold?

The liveryman used a chisel to free him from the chains. Slocum stood again, feeling his arms and legs. Would he ever be able to walk again without pain? He was lucky he hadn't broken anything during one of his falls.

"Jones," he said in a half whisper.

Addie tossed him a pair of boots and then shook a finger at him. "Don't you go gettin' no ideas 'bout revenge, John. We're gonna get the gold while all hell has cut loose."

"I don't even have a gun, Addie."

"Get him the gun," she said to the liveryman.

He gave Slocum a holster that was full of a Peacemaker. Addie picked up a shotgun. The smithy had a Winchester.

Slocum shook his head. "Y'all are *loco*."

Addie pointed to the back door. "It's like this, handsome. We know where the chest is. We can get there by the back alley. We've got horses ready to load up. We're gonna take that gold out of here and give it back to Gable. He'll reward us if we do."

Slocum saw the corners of her mouth turn down. She was lying. Addie had no intention of giving back the gold. But she did not want Gable's own man to suspect her double cross.

"We better hurry, Mrs. Hanson."

Addie gazed with narrow eyes at the tall rebel. "You ain't gonna quit on me now, are you, John?"

The damned gold had been bad luck all along. Yet Addie was dead set on having it. How could he say no to her after she had saved his salt pork?

"All right."

Addie kissed him quickly. "I knew I could count on you. Come on, we've got to push that wagon down the alley."

Slocum grimaced. "Wagon?"

The smithy threw open the back door of the stable. "Hurry up. I think the shooting has almost stopped."

Addie urged Slocum toward the alley. "We got to get through this, honey. Do the best you can."

Slocum staggered forward, gradually regaining his balance on tentative legs. When he emerged into the alleyway, he saw a buckboard wagon and three saddled horses. There was no team horse attached to the wagon.

"We can't get out of here on this wagon," Slocum said.

The liveryman came through the door leading a packhorse. "We aren't goin' on the wagon. Hold these reins while I get the rest of them."

He led two more pack animals into the shadows. Slocum held the reins, watching for Dunwood's men—if there were any left after the shooting. Slocum smiled to himself. He had broken Dunwood's neck by knocking him off the gallows. They were even now, the cage for the mayor's dead body.

The liveryman hitched one of the packhorses to the buckboard. "Okay, let's go."

Slocum still wasn't sure what they had in mind. He just sat on the buckboard next to Addie, holding the packhorses. The wagon moved forward, rolling slowly down the alley.

"Faster," Addie urged.

"It's too narrow, Mrs. Hanson."

The shooting started again from the street on the other side of the buildings. It sounded so close. Slocum drew his Peacemaker from the holster.

"Addie, honey, are you sure—"

"John, look out!"

Addie's eyes bulged when she saw the man with the pistol. He had burst out from nowhere to aim the weapon at her. Addie let go with a double blast of the shotgun. The man flew back, crashing into a rainbarrel.

"Good shot," Slocum said.

Addie made a frustrated noise. "Help me up."

The kick of the scatter-gun had knocked her onto the floor of the wagon. Slocum pulled her upright. She reached into the folds of her bosom and took out two shotgun shells.

"I like a woman who's ready," he told her as he glanced over his shoulder. "Let's get the hell out of here!"

"We're almost there."

Slocum looked at the saddle horses that also trailed the wagon. He could just grab one and go. Hadn't he experienced enough of the gold's hexing power? The day before, he had been locked in a cage because of the damned treasure.

"John!"

Pistol fire followed Addie's cry. Bullets slammed into the buckboard, missing Slocum and the woman. The shots had come from above.

Slocum saw the silhouette against the sky. The man aimed again, but when he pulled the trigger nothing happened. He said, "Damn," and started to load his pistol right there.

The tall man raised his Colt, but a rifle beat him to the punch. The man on the roof clutched his chest and tumbled over the side, hollering all the way down. Smoke curled out of the smithy's Winchester.

"Nice work," Addie said.

Slocum shook his head. "What the hell are we doin'?"

"Almost there," the liveryman said.

Addie patted his hand. "You'll see. It's gonna work."

More rifle shots from the street. Slocum gripped the butt of the Colt in his sore gun hand. Suddenly the wagon stopped.

"We're here," Addie said.

Slocum glanced to his right. He recognized the back entrance of Dunwood's office. The late mayor wouldn't be needing his gold.

Gable's man levered a round into the Winchester. "I'm goin' up. You wait down here for me."

He opened the back door.

"No!" Slocum cried.

A rifle exploded inside the stairwell. The stableman's body buckled and he fell backward, bleeding from the chest. Slocum had figured there would be somebody on duty, guarding the gold.

"You're never gonna get this gold, rebel," a voice cried from the second story. "You hear me, worm bait?"

Slocum's eyes narrowed. "The kid."

Addie grabbed him. "No, let's get out of here. We don't need the gold."

"This ain't about the gold," Slocum replied. "I got Dunwood. Now I'm gonna get Hud Jones."

The kid was going to die for the cage.

25

Slocum rolled off the back of the wagon, taking Addie with him. He pulled her around to the other side. They lay there for a moment, listening. No sounds from the kid. Jones was probably holed up in the office, sitting on top of the gold.

"How are you going to get him?" Addie asked. "How do we even know that Gable's men will win that fight in the street?"

"Hush up."

His green eyes scanned the barrels under the windows, where he had stood several times during his eavesdropping. If he could get the angle on the kid, he could shoot him. It had to be quick. Addie was right—the battle in the street wouldn't last forever.

Slocum gazed toward the back door again. "Addie, when I give you the signal, shoot that doorway with your scatter-gun. Once, then again."

"What?"

"Just watch me and do it!"

Slocum crawled away from her, moving around toward the front of the buckboard. He looked up at the windows for a moment. He didn't see the kid there. Rising to his feet, he scuffled toward the barrels and crates that rested against the wall.

He gazed back at Addie, who was watching him as ordered. Slocum took a deep breath and waved his hand. Addie unleashed one barrel of the scatter-gun into the door.

Immediately, the kid answered the shotgun blast with a barrage of rifle fire. Slocum used the noise of the commotion to hide the sound of his climbing. When he made it to the top, he listened carefully by the open window.

The kid was reloading. Slocum could hear the metallic clicking of the cartridges as they went into the Winchester. Easing his face up to the sill, Slocum peered into the dim office. The shadows were too thick for him to see Jones. He ducked down again.

Addie still had her gaze locked on him. He waved at her again. She blasted the entrance with the second barrel.

As soon as Jones began to shoot, Slocum raised up and fixed the kid's position. The barrel of the Winchester spat smoke and fire. Slocum put the Colt through the opening, taking aim at Jones, who was braced against the far wall of the room. Slocum didn't intend to miss with the first one. The kid had to pay for keeping him captive, for torturing him like a wild animal.

"Jones!" Slocum cried.

He wanted to see the kid's face, to see that moment of recognition when he knew Slocum had him. Jones froze for a moment. He started to swing with the Winchester. Slocum fired a single shot into his throat.

The kid quivered, grabbing at his neck. He staggered toward the window, but he never made it. His body lurched to the left, crashing down the stairwell. He rolled on his side, trying to get to his feet.

Addie's shotgun burst again. She finished the kid with a shot to the head. The load of buckshot blew away most of his crown. Blood and chunks of brain spattered the lower rung of steps.

Slocum didn't waste any time getting through the window. He saw that the gold was still in the saddlebags he had brought from the livery. Larceny came into his heart. His head jerked toward the door. There was nothing between him and stealing the gold.

A shadow appeared at the top of the stairs. Slocum pointed the Peacemaker at the shape. Addie told him to put the gun down.

Slocum lowered the barrel of the .45. "Here it is."

Addie rushed over to look at the saddlebags. "I knew we could do it. I'm sorry that nice liveryman had to die, but I enjoyed killing that other son of a bitch."

"I shot him first," Slocum said.

Addie picked up one of the saddlebags, barely lifting it from the floor. "Come on, help me."

"What're you doin'?"

She hauled the pouch of double eagles toward the window. "Just watch. The stable man figured it out."

Slocum assisted her, dragging the bag to the casement. "Now what?"

Addie hiked her thumb toward the window. "Out!"

"You're *loco*, woman."

"Easier'n totin' 'em down the stairs," she replied. "I told you, the boy there figured it out."

Despite Slocum's objections, they lifted the saddlebag and launched it toward the bed of the buckboard wagon. The bag hit the pile of hay in the back of the vehicle. It bounced and landed harmlessly on the cushion of straw.

"Damn," Slocum said. "It worked."

They repeated the process until the saddlebags were all gone.

"Let's get the hell out of here," Addie said.

Slocum shook his head. "I'm goin' alone."

Addie glared at him. "You promised me," she said.

"I'm breakin' my promise," he replied.

She raised the shotgun, which had been reloaded from her bra. "I saved your ass twice. And you promised to take me with you. You swore on the honor of Dixie."

He grimaced. He had done that. It was the only oath that he could never take back. She had him.

"On the honor of Dixie!" she repeated.

Slocum started for the door. "I know. Come on, let's get goin'. We ain't got all day."

The only sound was their heels on the stairs. No more shooting from the street. Had things really calmed down?

Slocum emerged from the building with his Colt leading the way. He heard movement on his right. A man stood there with a pistol in his hand.

"Don't move," the man said.

Addie came out behind Slocum.

The man's eyes turned to the woman. "Whoa, little—"

Slocum wheeled with his Colt, discharging it in the man's chest. The *pistolero* fell to the ground. And Slocum's shot set off the skirmish in the street again. More gunfire echoed through Rock Springs.

"Get those bags onto the horses!" Addie cried.

Slocum had to catch the animals. They were still tied up but the gunfight had them skittish. He finally put the saddlebags on two packhorses and one bag each on their mounts.

"That way," Addie said, pointing to the end of the alley.

"Can you ride?" Slocum asked.

She swung into the saddle like a champ. "Can you?"

Slocum mounted a tall black gelding. He felt dizzy in the saddle. Shapes spun before his eyes.

Addie squinted at him. "Are you okay?"

Slocum nodded. Nothing was going to stop him from having the gold. He spurred the gelding forward. The animal lurched into a run.

"Easy!" Addie cried.

She rode behind him with the pack animals, trying to catch up.

Slocum reeled and teetered in the saddle. Something had worn off. He no longer had the edge inside him. And the pain was starting to come back stronger.

"Cowboy, look out!"

At the end of the alley, a rifleman was taking aim at Slocum. The tall man lifted his Colt and fired. He missed, but it didn't matter. He rode right past the rifleman, who also fell short of the mark.

Addie also rushed by the rifleman, who didn't seem to be able to hit anything. She gazed ahead at Slocum. The tall man had cleared the town, digging for the river.

"Wait!" she cried.

Slocum reined back a little on the strong gelding. He glanced over his shoulder to see Addie on his tail. He had to drop back to help her.

"John!" Addie cried. "There!"

Slocum finally saw the rider coming out of the east. He cocked the hammer of his Colt again, firing as soon as the intruder was close enough. The man also had a pistol. Slocum had to shoot three times to kill him.

They drove hard again toward the river. Addie kept looking back to see if there were any more riders. Smoke billowed over the roofs of Rock Springs. Somebody had started a fire, which meant that a posse was unlikely.

"East!" Slocum cried in his haze.

Addie shook her head and pointed to the south. "That way."

What the hell did she have in mind? Slocum felt the sweat pouring down his face. He wondered how much longer he would be able to keep his eyes open.

"It's not far," Addie said.

Slocum turned with her, heading straight toward a rocky rise. He almost fell from the saddle a couple of times. He had to trust the woman because there wasn't much strength left in him. Would she save his life yet a third time?

A pain began to burn in his throat. Sweat salted the rope wound. He had been right there, looking toward the light of the beyond. Addie's loving hand had pulled him back.

"Hang on, John!"

Slocum didn't see why they were heading for the rise. It was all rock. No place to go, no way to escape.

"We're almost there."

Surely a posse would not come after them—nobody knew about the gold. Except Gable, so he might be looking for them. But it was doubtful that a posse would come from the town.

"That way," Addie said, pointing between two boulders.

They took the horses into a narrow ravine. It was a dead end. Slocum thought she had ridden him into a trap.

"Addie—"

"It's okay, honey."

She reined up and climbed out of the saddle. "Can you get down, John? Dismount for me, honey."

Slocum tried to lean over, but he lost his balance. Addie broke his fall a little, but he still hit the ground hard. His head boiled with a fever. He was growing weaker and weaker by the second.

"Addie—"

"Shh, don't die on me, handsome. We come too far for that. Here, can you make it up the path?"

They trod across bare rock, toward a wall of sheer stone. Slocum thought she had gone mad. Then Addie drew back the piece of dead brush, revealing the opening in the wall.

"In here," she said. "It's an old mine."

Another trap? Why had she brought him here? Slocum hesitated. He would not go into the mine shaft.

"What's this?" he said with quivering lips.

"I told you, it's an old mine. We can hide out here till everything has calmed down. Go in."

"How? When?"

She shook her head. "If you ain't the orneriest—I was busy while you were in jail," she said. "Now come on."

They had to crawl into the small opening. Addie went first so she could help him through. Slocum lay belly down on the cool floor of the mine. When Addie struck a match and lit an oil lamp, he saw that she had stored in supplies—food, blankets, and water.

"How?" he asked. "How'd you—"

She sighed. "You alway sell me short, cowboy. I got more tricks than a raccoon with two peckers. Come on, let's get you under these blankets."

She had arranged a pallet on the floor of the cave, stacks of blankets and quilts. Slocum stretched out, closing his eyes. He wondered if he was going to die. His whole body roasted with the fever.

Addie dabbed a wet cloth on his forehead. "You're gonna be all right. I swear it. I'm not gonna let you die."

"Whiskey," Slocum said. "Please."

"Sure, honey. I got whiskey."

Slocum did not see her pour the powder into the booze. She lifted the cup to his mouth. Slocum wondered why the whiskey tasted bitter. It made him feel better almost immediately.

"Gold," he muttered in a low voice.

"Don't worry," Addie said. "I got a place to hide the horses and the gold. When I get finished, I'll be back to tend you."

Slocum closed his eyes. "Thanks."

"Oh, Johnny boy, I'm sorry."

But he didn't hear her. Instead, he drifted off into a slumber that was filled with light. He came in and out of the sleep periodically and the woman always hovered before his eyes. She was good. Like an angel.

The sleep was restful as a lazy summer day when he was a boy, fishing for catfish on the Chattahoochee River back in Georgia.

Birds filled the air, singing. A tug on his line. Music from his cousin's harmonica. And always the light. He didn't care much if he died. He just wanted to stay in the glow of the light.

26

Slocum opened his green eyes to see shapes dancing above him on a ceiling of uneven rock. He had descended into hell. The orange glow was the reflection from the fires of Satan. The tall man wanted to scream but he found that his mouth was cotton dry.

"No."

He sat up. There were no fires. Just a single oil lamp burning on top of a crude footstool. Slocum was still in the cave.

How had he gotten there? And how long had he been out? His head ached but most of the other pain had left him.

"Rock Springs," he muttered to himself.

Some of it came back. The woman, the fighting. They had ridden out of town after a lot of trouble. It had all started on a stagecoach.

Slocum wanted to stand up. He tried his legs, which were weak but strong enough to hold him. He staggered a few steps forward. At least he hadn't died along the way.

His mouth needed something wet. He found a jug of water and lifted it to his lips. The cool liquid eased the burning in his mouth and throat.

He had faded in and out of sleep. The woman had been there. Where was she now? Slocum squinted in the dim light.

The oil lamp had burned low. It was almost out of fuel. Slocum turned up the wick a little. It was then that he saw the note attached to the stool.

173

The paper carried the scent of Addie Hanson.

"Damn her."

She had bolted.

"The gold!" Slocum said.

He remembered the saddlebags full of double eagles. Addie had stolen it from him. Then she had left him to die.

"Never shoulda trusted her."

Slocum sat on the floor of the cave, unfolding the piece of perfumed paper. Addie's handwriting was long and flowing, not what he would suspect from a girl who worked under the sheets. Slocum began to read what she had written.

"Dear John: It's been five days now since we escaped from Rock Springs. I don't know if you are going to live or die. The truth is, I've done all I can and I can't take you back into Rock Springs. They might lynch you if they got hold of you again."

Slocum shook his head. "Always lookin' out for my welfare. What a girl. Always savin' me."

"I love you, John. That I'm sure of. But love doesn't matter much to a woman in my place. I've got to watch out for myself, handsome. If you look close, you'll know I'm right."

Slocum sighed. She had a point. Were they really any different, the two of them? He would have run out on her sooner or later. Addie had simply beaten him to the draw.

"I've gone with Gable," the letter went on. "He's a nice man. I hope we get married. He found me, John, and he wanted to hurt you. But I wouldn't let him. I told him to leave you alone."

"Saved me again."

"I hope you recover to read this, handsome. I gave you all the powder that I had. I ran out of whiskey too. So I just left you here. I figured you're the kind of man who wants to die alone. Or live alone."

He shook his head. The woman had really known him. Or was it that she just knew men in general?

There was still more in her elegant hand.

"I didn't let Gable take all the gold, John. Check your boot."

Slocum's boots were sitting next to the footstool. He reached inside the left one to find his Peacemaker. A leather pouch came out of the right boot. Slocum opened the pouch, pouring ten gold coins into his hand.

"There's two hundred dollars here," said Addie's farewell note. "I figured you had it coming, since you were never paid that money owed to you for riding shotgun. I hope you live to see this."

Slocum nodded. Addie had done right by him, even if she had left him to die. He almost felt sad that she was gone. He stuffed the pouch into his pants pocket.

"If you are alive, John, there's a horse up the ravine. He's saddled. I left oats and there's some water there. I left jerky for you and some dried beans in case you ride on the trail. Even if you are in heaven, honey, please forgive me for what I have done."

Forgive and forget, Slocum thought. It wasn't always easy. He suspected that Addie had been in collusion with Gable, but at least she had tried to keep him from dying.

"Addie girl, Addie girl. What am I gonna do with you? Nothin'. That's all I'm gonna do with you," he wondered aloud.

She had signed the letter, "Ever loving you, Adelaide."

Slocum stared at the letter for a moment. It seemed so final. He held it over the lamp until it caught fire and disappeared into ashes.

Five days in the cave. Or at least five days until Addie had abandoned him. He might have slept even longer.

There was no need to get upset over what had been, he decided. It was best just to take the bull by the horns. He pulled on his boots.

His holster lay on the other side of the stool. Slocum strapped it on and slid the Peacemaker into the leather. He pulled the weapon out immediately, checking the cylinder which carried five shots, then dropped it back on his side.

Addie had even left him a hat. It was a round, white Stetson with a narrow brim. Slocum never would have chosen the hat for himself, but it was clean and it fit so he decided to wear it.

"What else did you squirrel away, Addie girl?"

He found the dried meat. His stomach called for something filling. Slocum took huge bites, eating with an appetite for the first time in a week.

A bedroll was next on the list. He rolled up the blankets and quilts from the floor. He was starting to feel normal again. If he could just stay out of trouble for a little while.

He had to find the horse. Crawling through the opening, he followed Addie's directions to the black gelding that had taken him out of Rock Springs. The animal's snout was half submerged in a pool of runoff water. True to the woman's word, the mount had been saddled. There was even a canteen hanging from the saddle horn.

How had she forced Gable to give up so much?

Slocum just laughed to himself. Addie's inclination toward womanly persuasion had no equal. She could talk the Devil out of his pitchfork.

Leading the black down the path, he stopped again at the adit of the mine shaft. Crawling back in, he pushed his meager belongings out into the sunlight. He took everything but the stool and the lamp.

When the gelding was loaded, he mounted up and started out of the rocks. As soon as he hit level ground, he drove hard to the east. He was going to follow the river south.

The air was cool as it rushed over Slocum. Somehow it felt right to be in the saddle again. Like all the bad luck had passed. If he could just get south with the money, he could let Rock Springs fade in his memories.

Keep low.

No big towns.

Find a cantina in New Mexico.

Stay out of trouble.

He rode on, avoiding trouble for the next thirty minutes, but finding it again at the banks of the river.

Slocum did not approach the river by way of the main road. He came out of some rocks, which brought him without warning to the group of men in dusters. He immediately reined the black, stopping to stare at them. They looked back. Slocum was going to turn away, but he realized they had him surrounded.

A short, dark-haired man stepped toward him, tipping back a wide Stetson. "Howdy."

Slocum did not recognize the man. Had Gable brought in new hired guns? There seemed to be nine or ten of them circled around him.

"Where you headed, stranger?" the man asked.

Slocum shrugged. "South."

The short man nodded, drawing back the lapel of his duster to reveal a shiny tin star. "I'm Lucas Garry, territorial marshal."

Slocum took a deep breath. His heart went wild. He had ridden right into the rattler's nest.

"Been up Rock Springs way," the marshal said. "Trouble there. You know anythin' about it?"

Slocum shook his head. "No."

The marshal peered suspiciously at the tall man. "Where you comin' from anyway, stranger?"

"Nowhere."

"Hey," one of the other men said, "he's the Sheriff from over at Rock Springs. Looks just like him."

The marshal glanced at his man. "Sheriff?"

"Sure, I was through Rock Springs when the sheriff had killed some badass, what was his name? Some big miner— Bateman, I think. Killed three of 'em. That mayor had the bodies out in the street."

Marshal Garry gestured at Slocum. "Maybe you oughta climb on down here for a minute, pardner."

Slocum made a coughing sound. "I ain't no sheriff, mister. Look at me. Go on. Do I look like a sheriff?"

Another voice rose from the ring of men. "Aw, he ain't no sheriff. Let him be, Marshal."

Garry cast a sideways glance at the loudmouth. "Let me be the judge of this. What is your name, sir?"

Slocum sighed. "John. John Slocum."

"See if we have any posters on a man named John Slocum," Garry said over his shoulder.

Slocum thought he was sunk. There was no way he could take on this many guns. He couldn't remember if there were any posters on him in southern Wyoming.

The marshal eyed him closely. "Maybe you'd like to tell me again where you're ridin' from?"

Slocum eyed him right back. "Truth is, marshal, I got sick on the trail. I been lyin' in a cave for a week. I don't know where I am or where I'm goin'. Maybe you'd be so kind as to point me south."

"No posters on him," called a voice from the ring of men.

Garry sighed. "I guess you ain't done nothin' wrong in my jurisdiction. Hell, you're about the only one these days."

"I still say he looks like that sheriff from Rock Springs," cried the persistent deputy. "I saw him plain as day."

"What about this?" Garry asked.

Slocum shifted in the saddle. "Do I look like a sheriff to you? Huh? Who'd hire me as sheriff?"

"They coulda been twins—"

"Hush," Garry replied to his man.

Slocum figured to play it out, something he had learned from Addie. "I could use some work myself, Marshal. I'm honest." The double eagles suddenly felt heavy in his pockets.

"I'm afraid I can't help you there," Garry replied.

The eager lawman wouldn't be quiet. "I tell you, that's the sheriff. Take him into Rock Springs. You'll see. Let them identify him."

"The sheriff was killed in that fire," somebody said. "They found the body in the ashes."

Garry put his hands on his hips, glaring at the tall man. "Maybe it wouldn't be a bad idea to ride him back into Rock Springs."

A sweat broke on Slocum's brow. He had ridden right into the fire. Everybody in Rock Springs would be able to identify the face of Brick Hanson, the man who had hidden away the gold in the mountains.

"Aw, let's get back home, marshal," someone said from the ring of men.

"Yeah, it's been a long ride."

"He ain't no sheriff."

"Look at him, he's a trail bum."

Slocum smiled and nodded. "That's me. I could use a grub-stake boys. Anybody got a dollar or two bits?"

Garry laughed. "Yeah, they say Hanson stashed all that gold hereabouts. And you don't appear to be a rich man."

"Four bits," Slocum said. "Help a *hombre* out, boys."

But nobody had a heart full of charity, which suited Slocum just fine. He didn't want to take any money from lawmen. The beggar ruse had worked.

Marshal Garry climbed into the saddle of his own mount. "I guess we will head home."

"That's the sheriff, Marshal!"

"Hush up, Sherman." Garry looked at Slocum and smiled. "He's new. You got to excuse him."

"No offense taken," Slocum said.

Garry laughed and shook his head. "Yessiree, you sure as shootin' don't look like a sheriff to me, Mr. Slocum. You could never be a lawman."

The tall man from Georgia took off his hat and made a horseback version of a southern gentleman's sweeping bow. "Thank you kindly, Marshal Garry. You don't know how glad I am to hear you say that."

Slocum donned his hat and pushed through the line of men, guiding the black gelding along the riverbank to freedom.

EPILOGUE

A hot summer sun beat down on Slocum's dirty white hat. He had come south to find the heat and he had not been disappointed. His two-month trek had brought him down a meandering course that left him broke and tired. He only had two double eagles remaining from the gold that the woman had given him. Where had it all gone? To whiskey, whores, gambling, and grub. He had also traded horses along the way, getting rid of the gelding. A horse trader had given him fifty dollars and a sorrel mare for the black.

But the fifty was also gone and the mare was on her last legs. He had to trade her, though he doubted that he could even give her away. Maybe some Mexican would buy the mare for a plow horse.

Slocum figured he was somewhere near Raton. He had come down a long pass, emerging in thin woods. The trail was well-worn, so he knew he was getting close to a settlement. Slocum had been to Raton before, a place where whiskey was easily found.

Sure enough, the sun-beaten jerkwater town appeared before him, promising yet another place to spend the last of his money. He had not worked along the way. And he had stopped at too many places. The damned double eagles just drew a man to an easier way of living. He had to work again to get the rich man's demons out of his head.

Nobody took much notice of his arrival. He stopped in front of the saloon and tied up the mare. When he entered the place, he was surprised to see that it was not half bad. It was clean and it didn't have the usual goat-smell to it. There was also a sign that said "Free Lunch" in back of the bar. Despite that claim, the saloon was empty.

Slocum eased up to the bar. He took off his hat and ran his hands over his head. It almost felt good to be in a town. Then again, he couldn't wait to get back on the trail. It was a strange way to be.

He took out a double eagle and slapped it down on the bar. "Anybody in here?"

"Pick up your money, John Slocum. It's no good here."

The tall man squinted into the shadows. "Who knows me?"

A woman sashayed behind the bar. "You don't mean to tell me that you've forgotten your own wife. Have you, *Sheriff*?"

His mouth fell open. "Addie Hanson!"

"How are you, handsome?"

Slocum lifted a finger to point at her. "You left me to die," he said, scowling at her.

She grimaced and waved him off. "You made it. I knew you would. And I left you set up. Hell, Gable wanted to take you back into town and hang you himself."

Slocum touched the scar on his neck. She had saved his life a couple of times. Maybe it was best to forgive and forget.

"I'm the first to say I'm sorry," Addie went on. "We had the gold and I let Gable talk me out of it. I thought he wanted to marry me, but he didn't."

Slocum's brow furrowed. "How the hell did you get here?"

Addie sighed and shrugged. "How did *you* get here?"

"What happened with Gable?"

She smirked and shook her head. "You know what he wanted me to do? He wanted me to whore for him. Bring in girls for the men who were working on the railroad. He wanted me to work too."

"That still don't tell me how you got here."

Addie made a circling motion with her wrist. "Round and round."

Slocum grinned at her. "You kept some of that gold for yourself, didn't you? How much?"

"Just one saddlebag," she replied.

Slocum held out his hand. "Give it to me."

"Give you what?" she said with indignation.

"My share."

Addie shook her head. "No, uh-uh, all that money is in a bank in Denver, drawing interest for my old age."

"What about this place?"

"Well, my stage broke down here, so I was hanging around. The old man who owned the saloon before me was half-dead. You might say I made his last days more . . . joyful. He left me this place. And I been doin' pretty good."

Slocum laughed. "It figures. Can I at least have a few days of food and whiskey? On the house?"

She raised her eyebrows. "You can have more'n that. There's a bed upstairs. Why don't you go up and wait for me?"

"Why not?"

He climbed up to a bedroom that smelled of Addie's unforgettable perfume. For a moment, he was taken back to all that had happened. But he couldn't dwell on it for long. It was better to just forget some things, like iron cages and hangman's nooses.

Slocum took off his clothes and climbed into the bed. He would take Addie for a tumble, wait around a couple of days until he could steal something from her. He had to extract his due. They had been in on the gold together, so it was his rightful debt to claim.

Rest up. Steal as much as possible. She owed him. *Or did she?* What had his life been worth? She had saved him. How could he feel resentment?

The trail sure took some baffling turns. He wouldn't steal. Couldn't steal.

Addie came in and dropped her housecoat. She climbed in, rubbing against his body. They began to sweat in the summer heat.

When they were finished, Addie put her head on his moist chest. "You can stay," she said. "Share it all."

Slocum didn't like the sound of that. He told her to go to sleep. They both nodded off for a while.

Slocum awoke in the late afternoon, thinking that he had better move along. But then Addie shifted next to him and they both sank into the middle of the bed. When he felt her warm skin and drew in that deadly perfume, the tall man from Georgia started trying to convince himself that it might not be a bad idea to spend a few more days in Raton.

A special offer for people who enjoy reading the best Westerns published today.

WESTERNS!

NO OBLIGATION

Mail the coupon below

To start your subscription and receive 2 FREE WESTERNS, fill out the coupon below and mail it today. We'll send your first shipment which includes 2 FREE BOOKS as soon as we receive it.